APLEY TOWERS

The Lost Kodas

Myra King

Sweet Cherry

Publishing

Sweet Cherry
Publishing

Published by Sweet Cherry Publishing Limited
Unit E, Vulcan Business Complex
Vulcan Road
Leicester, LE5 3EB
United Kingdom

www.sweetcherrypublishing.com

First published in the UK in 2015
ISBN: 978-1-78226-277-0

Illustrations © Creative Books
Illustrated by Subrata Mahajan
Cover design and illustration by Andrew Davis

Apley Towers: The Lost Kodas

Printed and bound by Thomson Press India Ltd.

For Shannon: who never reads but always listens.
And Kael: who always reads but never listens.

"And though she be but little, she is fierce."
                              - William Shakespeare

❧ Prologue ❧

The land reminded her of the English woodlands, the ones whose borders she had spent her childhood on. But she knew that was crazy. She had learnt the hard way that South Africa wasn't like her motherland.

"The stables are all in good condition. Just need a coat of paint, I suppose," the man said.

The woman could not believe her luck. After all of the trouble she'd had recently, how had she stumbled so magically on this place?

"Are you sure this is all included? All of this land?" she asked tentatively, surveying the sleepy meadows.

"Yes ma'am. All of it," the man answered, and after a moment's hesitation added, "you're not from around here, are you?"

"No," she said a little sadly, "I'm from England. I came to South Africa with my husband … Ex-husband," she quickly corrected.

"So what will you be wanting with all this land, then?"

"A riding school," she said with a tinge of hope, "that was always the dream."

She could see it as though it already existed: a paddock for grazing, three riding rings, a tack room and, in the distance, her own little house nestled amongst the giant oak trees. It would be her own little paradise, concealed from the world. She could imagine life and laughter in this place. She could imagine a second chance at happiness.

"I'll take it."

"Excellent, why don't we go over to the house and start the paperwork?"

As the woman drew nearer to her future home, she gave a cry of surprise.

"Oh there are two chimneys. They look like towers on either side of the house."

"I really do love your accent," the man said with a chuckle, "which part of England are you from?"

"Shropshire. I grew up in a tiny village called Apley. This place sort of reminds me of the woods."

"Have you decided what you are going to name your riding school?"

The woman looked across her property, her paradise.

"Apley Towers," she said with confidence. "This will be Apley Towers."

✌ One ☙

Gravel crunched loudly under Kaela Willoughby's riding boots as she bounced down the little dirt road. She glanced back over her shoulder at the path she had already walked – she wondered just how many times she had walked the half-mile from her house to the Apley Towers stable in her life.

"Probably a thousand," she said to the wind. "Am I a thousand days old? Let's see, I'm fourteen and five months now, so ..."

Kaela squared her eyes as a jumble of numbers danced across her brain. She frowned at her boots and her shadow looked up at her, silently laughing.

"Oh I give up, I have no idea. This is why I'm not a mathematician. There are more interesting things in life." On the ground, her shadow seemed to beckon to the stable

7

and she needed to be on her way. She smiled at it and resumed walking, "Such as riding."

On the path ahead of her, dandelion seeds danced in the wind. She followed them, making wishes for each one as she passed.

The South African summer sun blazed down; the air was humid and choking.

"January is always the hottest month of summer," she told her shadow.

In the distance, through the wooden fence, Kaela got her first glimpse of the stable. The horseflies buzzed in lazy drones around the paddock whilst mares and geldings swished at them with long, wiry tails. The occupants of the stable, both equine and human, were straining in the heat.

The humans were not as lucky as the lazing horses. The work never ended. There were always stalls to muck out, horses to groom, tack to clean, things to fix, food and hay to be distributed. Stable grooms took it in turns to run their heads under the taps to cool themselves down. In this heat, a constant supply of cold water was vital. A groom walked the length of the stable throwing ice cubes in the water buckets. Kaela spotted him munching on a cube to keep himself cool too. She knew that the calm look of the stables was temporary. It only appeared to be well ordered and serene from a distance. Up close, it was an entirely different story.

Once through the Apley Towers gate, the chaos of the property engulfed her. Riders – mostly girls, mostly children

– bustled around in their humdrum of noise, laughter, panic and horse-driven insanity. It was loud, but it was the usual craziness. It was normal for Kaela now.

After avoiding Jeremy the donkey, who was intent on chasing every car out of the car park, she reached the stables. She dodged the plethora of little girls in hard hats, and gave the dogs a soft pat in the hope that it would stop their barking. It didn't.

She loved Apley. Despite the hard work, she could never get enough of this place. Wendy Oberon, her instructor and the stable owner, had always said that for one hour in the saddle, two had to be spent working in the stable. Kaela took this saying very seriously and always arrived an hour before her lesson to do her bit. Today was no different.

"And, tell us Miss Willoughby," Joseph, a groom, said as he walked by leading two horses, "how was the very first day of the brand new school year? Was it worth the tantrum you had yesterday?"

"I still maintain that my boot took itself off and threw itself across the feeding paddock on its own."

"I'm sure it did," Joseph said with a chuckle.

"And actually, it was worth the tantrum. Six weeks off celebrating summer and Christmas, only to be thrown back into a classroom. When will I find time to write and ride? Shakespeare never had to deal with this."

"That he didn't," the groom led the horses on.

Kaela smiled as Joseph disappeared. She made her way to the tack room, grabbed a rogue curry brush and found one of the waiting horses. She would occupy her time with grooming until someone gave her more important instructions. That was the way of the stable, you never knew when a crazed and over-worked adult would come spiralling at you with obscure requests. She entered Rhapsody's stall and began sweeping the dust from his back in large strokes. There was no better sound in the world. She breathed in and smiled.

"Kaela," a voice cried, bringing her out of her daydream.

She looked over to see Wendy, her normal neat hair now wild around her face, her make-up starting to run. After more than sixteen years in South Africa, she still hadn't got used to the heat.

"Yes?"

"I know this is last minute but would you please teach the beginners' class?" Wendy smiled pleadingly.

"Of course."

The stable owner let out a sigh of relief.

"Nothing too strenuous, just put the girls through their paces."

"I'll keep it easy, I promise."

"Thanks Kae, you're a life saver. I knew I could trust you with the beginners," she said, and walked off in a hurry.

Kaela smiled proudly and went back to grooming. She could already hear the grooms tacking the horses for the beginners' class. She knew the drill so well that she could recognise every action by the melody of its sound.

Apley Towers had become an extension of herself through the years; what happened at the stable happened at her core.

"Hello Kae," Derrick, the head groom, said as he put Rhapsody's saddle on the door and threw the reins over it. "So how was the first day of school? Can you believe the Christmas holidays went by so fast?"

"I know, I feel like we broke up for the summer only a week ago."

Kaela thought of the alarm clock going off too early, of the heat as she sat in the stuffy classrooms whilst being told how to wrap the books and files she would need for the forthcoming year. It was the same speech every year.

Kaela repressed the need to roll her eyes at the memory of the day.

"It was okay. It's hard to get back into the swing of things after six weeks off. At least we didn't get any homework," at least, she didn't think she did.

"I hear you're teaching the class. Wanna quickly get Rhapsody tacked, then head down to the ring?"

"Will do," Kaela said, and grabbed the saddle and bridle.

Once Rhapsody was fully tacked and awaiting his rider, she made her way to the beginners' ring. She had to walk past all the beginners' horses; eight tacked horses in all meant a full class. The cool stables and calm of the dozy horses ended as soon as Kaela got to the riding rings. The sun seeped down on her, burning her skin even through her clothes.

Kaela rubbed the back of her burning neck. She tried to push the noise of the stables out of her ears for a moment.

This section of the school was separated into three rings. The first ring was for the beginners: it was square with nothing but trotting poles in the middle. The second ring was for the intermediates: it was rectangular with three-foot jumps as well as other obstacles the intermediate rider may encounter. The last ring was a trap of six-foot jumps as well as semi-gorges, trees, barrels, posts, rubber tyres, and anything else to test the advanced rider's abilities. Kaela brought her attention to the tables surrounding the rings: tired mothers sat watching their daughters as they zipped around the horses' legs. Kaela frowned at the scene, as she always did. Her mother had never sat at those tables. She pushed that thought out of her mind and walked into the ring.

Eight little girls with five fat ponies and three fat horses struggled to mount. They couldn't get their little feet in the high stirrups, and those that could were not strong enough to grip the saddle and pull themselves up. Derrick rushed between the horses, lifting the girls and getting their stirrups to a safe length. Kaela went forward to help, but stopped as soon as she caught sight of the brown-haired, school uniform clad young man who stood between two ponies and adjusted stirrups.

"How do you know so much about riding, Bart?" a little girl asked.

"Because, I have been riding since I was one year old. So I've been riding for fifteen years."

He lifted the last girl and began adjusting her stirrups.

"That's a long time to ride," she said.

"That's what happens when your mother owns a stable."

He smiled at the girls and then caught sight of Kaela. He lifted his eyebrows, bringing a smile to her face.

"Mum said you needed a bit of help today."

Kaela, unable to speak for the moment, merely nodded. Not for the first time in her life, she noticed that Bart said the British word 'Mum' rather than the South African word 'Mom'. Whenever he did this, Kaela's stomach did a flip flop. The beautiful sound of the strange word only reminded her of how unique Bart was. Like a white rose, in a garden of red ones.

"All right, fabulous Miss Kae, they are all yours. Enjoy your lesson girls," Derrick grinned.

"Thank you," they chorused.

Bart smiled, gave the two nearest ponies a pat, and walked by Kaela. He held his hand up for a high five. With *enormous* effort, Kaela lifted her hand and touched it to his.

On the ground, her shadow appeared to be laughing.

Kaela ignored it and commanded the beginners to walk on.

Teaching the beginners was easy – make them walk, test their balance, make them trot. It wasn't much really, although the last fifteen minutes of the class was dedicated to testing them a little bit more. It helped those who were good enough to stand up to the challenge. For the others, it was fun to watch.

As Kaela had all the riders drop their reins and swing their arms from side to side without losing their seat, she heard a ruckus coming from the stable. She turned in time to see Beatrix King, her best friend, drop the three saddles she was carrying. This sight was not an unfamiliar one to Kaela, who often witnessed her friend hoarding three saddles, four bridles, two crops and anything else she could tuck between her fingers, across the stables. She caught sight of Kaela and waved, Kaela laughed and waved back.

"Are you tacking the intermediate horses?" she called.

"No, I'm headed out to Neverland."

"One day, someone is going to take you out and blame the backchat!"

"Until then, I'll be in Neverland," Trixie grinned and disappeared into a stall.

Kaela brought her attention back to the class, where the girls trotted around her without much trouble.

"Michelle, heels down. Kirsten, double bounce, you're posting on the wrong leg. Shanaeda, grip with your calves and not your knees, sit deeper in the saddle. Jane, you are too stiff, loosen up or you're going to accidentally nudge the horse into a canter."

Riding was hard, there was so much to remember and so much you had to do. It was any wonder that anyone actually enjoyed it.

"What is Jeremy doing?" Jane suddenly called, looking anxiously behind her.

Kaela looked over and there, to her immense shock, was Jeremy the donkey trotting along behind the last horse.

"He has joined the lesson, I think." Kaela laughed.

"He must have run out of cars to attack!" one of the girls said.

The girls all giggled and squealed as the riderless donkey kept up with the class.

"Stupid donkey," Kaela said under her breath. With the girls laughing and not concentrating, someone was liable to get hurt.

"Get out of there, you crazy old man!" Derrick cried.

He was in the saddle of an advanced horse. He joined the class, riding up alongside Jeremy, and used his crop to shuffle him out of the ring. The little donkey jumped a fence nearly his own height.

"He could be a show jumper," Kaela cried.

"I know, what a surprise," Derrick said, "we should be using his talents."

He jumped his giant horse over the same fence, and chased Jeremy to a safe distance.

When the beginners' class was coming to a close, Kaela told the two lead riders to canter whilst the others dismounted. She watched as they cantered around the ring, both with big cheesy grins on their faces. They bounced in the saddle quite a bit, but other than that they were improving.

"Hey guys, grip with your calves and sit deeper in the saddle," she called. But it made no difference, the girls still bounced, "A canter is supposed to be smooth: move your pelvis in motion with the horse," she said.

It still made no difference. She would have to work on that next time.

Now that the class was over, the grooms came to the ring to lead the horses on an outride, which was something they did after every lesson to cool the horses down and prevent them from getting sick. They then helped the girls put their horses away.

Kaela raced over to the stalls, knowing she wouldn't have long before her own class started.

"Hello Trixie-True, take on too many saddles this time?" she asked when she reached her friend.

"On the contrary – not enough. If I'd had more I would have been properly balanced," she said with a smile.

"I'm sure. Are all the horses tacked?"

"All except Quiet Fire," she said as she adjusted the throat-lash on her own horse.

"Excellent, I'll be right back."

"You know that the only reason no one tacked him is because he's seventeen hands high, and as wide as he is tall," Trixie stuck her head out of the stall and called.

Kaela raced to the tack room to fetch Quiet Fire's saddle and bridle.

"He is too tall to get the saddle on without a footstool,

and too wide to get the girth on without a lot of huffing and puffing," Trixie continued as Kaela rushed past.

"I love a challenge," Kaela cried. "Hey, my boy," she said when she saw him. He desperately needed a groom, his black-blue coat was brown with dust. "I'll groom you after class."

Kaela began tacking him as fast as she could, she could already hear the horses walking to the ring. Luckily, she had put her riding hat in front of Quiet Fire's stall when she arrived. She grabbed it, led the horse out of the stable, and walked him to the ring. The tables were empty of mothers now; most lost interest after a few years of watching the horses go round in a circle, so the intermediates didn't get the pressure of many spectators.

Trixie had already mounted; she rode a chestnut gelding named Slow-Moe. Trixie was the only person who could get him to gallop. How she did it was a complete mystery, even to her. Kaela quickly mounted, set her stirrups right and prepared herself for class.

An hour later, Kaela hobbled back into the stable.

"Oh my aching calves," she moaned.

"Oh my aching rear end," Trixie moaned.

"If I wanted to ride without stirrups I would ride bareback," somebody else whimpered.

Wendy had made the class take their feet out of the stirrups and spend the next hour riding without them.

"Remind me to write a letter of complaint," another rider said whilst delicately dismounting.

It was only through sheer determination that Kaela was able to keep her promise to Quiet Fire. She untacked him with juddering arms, and groomed him with shaky legs. She was exhausted, and she still had to walk home to wrap files and books. She secretly wondered what would happen if she broke the rules and left her books unwrapped. Would she get the same lecture for the tenth time in her life?

Trixie finished grooming before Kaela as she had a smaller horse. She grabbed the hoof pick and helped her friend out. Neither spoke, both were preserving their energy for the trip home. But before the pair could finish, Wendy came up to the stall.

"May I please talk to you girls quickly?" she asked. She had given up and wiped the make-up off now, the irony being that the day had cooled so much that it would probably have held.

"Sure," they said in unison.

"I am going to Cape Town tomorrow, and will be there for a few days. Bart and Derrick are going to take care of the stable while I'm gone, but they can't do everything. Would the two of you be able to handle the beginners for a few days?"

"Us?" Kaela asked. "Really?"

"Yes, Derrick is too busy to teach and since I'm not around to pick Bart up from school, there is no guarantee that he will get here in time for the class. The pair of you can handle it. It will just be a repeat of today." Wendy smiled.

A cloud passed Trixie's face. She was never one for taking on more responsibility than she absolutely needed to. Kaela ignored her, as she usually did.

"Of course, we'd love to." Kaela exclaimed before Trixie even had a chance to think.

"Thanks a lot, you two are a huge help. Now hurry home before your parents get worried."

The girls finished grooming, said goodbye to everyone at the stable, and went their separate ways.

They didn't discuss what Wendy had asked of them.

❧ Two ❧

"Hey, do you want me to take the beginners today?" Kaela asked as the girls hung around the school grounds, waiting for the first bell to ring.

Trixie nodded, thinking it was only fair seeing as Kaela was the one to offer their help. Trixie did have to cycle home from school (in her school uniform – she had lost count of the amount of times the dress had been caught in the chain), and then she had to get changed and cycle over to Apley Towers. There was barely enough time for her to breath before her own class started.

"You might have to take all the classes," Trixie said, without looking up, "do you know who is going to be teaching the last two classes?"

"Probably Bart, who else can ride that well? I wonder why he isn't going to Cape Town with his mother?" Kaela said.

"He's got school."

Bart went to an all-boys school in the next town. The girls hardly ever got to see him outside of the stables.

Suddenly, Trixie looked away from the congregating students.

"Are your legs still sore?" she asked.

"No, I soaked myself in a hot salt-water bath last night and then–"

Trixie turned away after 'No'. When she asked a Yes/No question, she expected only a yes or no. She only had room in her head for the facts.

"What's our first class?" Trixie asked as she rummaged through her backpack, looking for her timetable.

"History," Kaela said with a smile, "one of the only two subjects I have any patience for."

"And then?"

"Science," she said and pulled a face, "one of two subjects I detest more than the rest."

"Brilliant, I love science," Trixie said with an excited smile. "Almost as much as I love maths."

Kaela lifted her eyebrow and snorted.

Not for the first time, Trixie wondered how she and Kaela managed to maintain such a close friendship. They were the exact opposite of each other.

The only thing they had in common was an obsession with all things equine.

Kaela raced down the hall, she was late for her meeting with the career advisor. She burst in as Mrs George sat down at her desk.

"Oh good, just in time!" Kaela said breathlessly.

"Actually five minutes late, but it's okay. Take a seat."

Kaela sat in the chair opposite the teacher. She hoped this wouldn't take long, she was late for another meeting too.

So far, the school year was going well …

"Kaela, I need to talk to you about your application for the J. M. Barrie Writing Course."

Kaela nodded. She had been waiting for this day. The J. M. Barrie Writing School offered a prestigious course taught by best-sellers and editors. It ran for a year, with one Saturday class on the beach per month.

It was expensive and illustrious; Kaela was desperate to get a place on it.

"Well, Kaela, I have been contacted by the school and asked to explain what is needed of you before they accept your application."

"What's needed of me?"

"Yes, unfortunately based on your first application, you cannot be accepted."

The words rounded on Kaela like a swarm of wasps, each syllable a harsh sting in her skin.

"Why not?" Kaela finally asked, trying to mask her disappointment.

"Because you are not the right type of student."

More wasp stings.

"According to them, your grades are not impressive and you are taking on too few extracurricular activities."

"Why does that matter to them? The course will be an extracurricular activity when I do it."

"They are not going to accept someone who can't prove they're capable of doing the work. You'll still be at school when you do the course, and usually they only take higher-education students and adults. They want to know you can take on everything they expect."

"Because I don't want to join the athletics team or do extra maths after school, they think I can't write?" Kaela tried to keep the edge out of her voice, but Mrs George still frowned. "What about my riding?" she added wistfully.

"I can't speak for them. I can just relate what they are saying. They're willing to let you resubmit the application though."

"Why?"

"Because of your essay. They see a lot of talent, and they can help you improve and move on to bigger things," Mrs George said with a smile.

"So why don't they just accept me?"

"It wouldn't be fair to applicants who do meet their standards."

Kaela felt hot tears sting her eyes.

But they are giving you another chance, she thought with hope.

She blinked back her tears, sniffed, and looked at the teacher.

"Okay, what do I need to do?"

"Are you up for the challenge?"

Kaela smiled hopefully, she had always loved a challenge.

"I'll take that as a yes. Okay, you need to work on your grades. Or you need to take part in more extracurricular activities."

"I can't. My afternoons are already fully booked with riding and the school newspaper."

"Well then, you are going to have to pull your grades up."

Kaela sighed, she had never been a good student. She had always just passed. Her teachers expected her to learn lines from the textbook and repeat them back exactly, and she expected to be able to question everything! She and the teachers clashed, and her marks suffered. "Doesn't riding count for anything?"

"Unfortunately not. But maybe you could take on a bit more responsibility at the newspaper."

"I suppose I could write more articles, or be more involved with the layout and printing."

"Not *or*, make it *and*. Do both. I think that will help. But do also try to pull your grades up."

"Okay, thanks for the help Mrs George."

"It is a pleasure, have a good afternoon. Oh and Kaela, I think it would be better if you prepared yourself for a rejection."

Kaela nodded sadly and walked out the classroom. Once outside, she started running for her other meeting.

She burst into that classroom and sat down.

"Thank you for joining us, Kaela," said Mr Keen, the history teacher.

"Sorry I'm late."

"Well you haven't missed much. I was just welcoming everyone back."

Kaela looked around the classroom, a few journalists from the year before were there. The rest were new, fresh-faced and nervous.

"As you already know, the editor and sub-editor have left our school now, so I would like some volunteers for new ones," Mr Keen said.

A girl in the front row quickly put her hand in the air and waved it around.

"But don't rush into this decision. The editor and sub-editor have to do a lot of work."

The girl's hand waved violently.

"And they have a lot of responsibility."

The girl's hand continued to wave.

"And they have to be very good at English, as they have to proofread everything."

The girl put her other hand in the air.

"Yes, Tessigan?" Mr Keen sighed and asked.

"I would like to be editor," Tessigan said, breathing heavily and grinning.

"Have you been waiting for this day since you joined the team?"

"No, since I started school."

The class laughed and Tessigan flushed.

"Yes okay, you can be editor. Are there any volunteers for a sub-editor?" Mr Keen asked. He looked around the classroom at the collection of students. Kaela noticed that Mr Keen's eyes never came to her.

Well, why would they? Kaela thought. *You've never volunteered for anything.*

Kaela thought about the requirements – a lot of work, a lot of responsibility, good at English. Could she slot herself into this mould? Kaela did a lot of work around the stables, always had. She had the responsibility of caring for the horses she rode. She also liked to think that she took care of her father. Not to mention, English was one of the subjects she could gladly say she was good at. Unlike everything else, she actually got good marks for it.

Should I volunteer? Kaela thought. *Could I?*

She slowly put her hand in the air.

"Yes, Kaela?"

"I'd like to volunteer for sub-editor."

Every face in the room turned to her in shock.

"You would like to be sub-editor? But what about your riding?" Mr Keen asked.

"I can do both." *Maybe.*

"Okay then," Mr Keen said slowly. He plastered a fake

27

smile on his face, turned to the class, and said, "Well, everybody say hello to your new editor and sub-editor."

"Hello," the journalists chorused.

Kaela had only a moment to doubt her decision before a tidal wave of questions made her push it quickly from her mind.

Trixie shoved her foot in the stirrup, grabbed the saddle, and lifted herself up. She swung her leg over and hooked her foot into the opposite stirrup.

"From the way she was acting, you would think I was some Amazon warrior about to attack her."

Kaela smiled, "I wish I had been an Amazon warrior and attacked her."

Trixie rolled her eyes at the memory of Mrs George and the difficult way she had handled their meeting that morning.

Kaela pulled Quiet Fire up to Slow-Moe and the two walked towards the ring, "So tell me again exactly what happened."

"So you know how we have to pick only six subjects which we'll carry through until the end of school? And you know how two of those subjects have to be languages because it is law? Well, I went to her to ask her why I had to take two languages, because there are more

than four other subjects I want to take. Which would mean I'm choosing seven subjects instead of six."

"What subjects do you want to take?" Kaela asked as she leaned down to open the gate.

"Well obviously the two languages, then maths, science, computer science, chemistry, and physics. Anyway, she argued with me that I can't take seven and that was the end of the discussion. Oh and then she asks me if I wouldn't rather want to be bilingual?"

"Well wouldn't you?"

"I'd rather know physics."

Kaela laughed as she closed the gate.

"So I asked her what the law was on taking seven subjects, and she says there is no law against it. So that settles it ... I'm taking seven subjects."

Kaela pulled Quiet Fire behind Slow-Moe and called, "That's a lot of subjects. Are you going to be okay with all that?"

"Of course," she leaned down to give Slow-Moe a pat, "we'll manage, won't we?"

Kaela logged into LetsChat and checked to see if anybody had left her any comments.

"One notification from *The Writer's Den*."

She clicked excitedly and waited for the page to load.

Can you still call yourself a writer if you've been rejected for a writing course? she thought.

Somebody named Phoenix White Feather had posted a question on the wall.

"Phoenix White Feather? That has got to be the most awesome name in existence."

Kaela read the question out loud to her father's empty study. The dark room was blissfully cool, and gave her hot, slightly burnt skin a moment to relax.

> **PWF:** *Help! I have to write the school play and although I have the whole story, I can't decide what to do with the ending? Do I have them live happily ever after, or do I have him board the alien ship and come back in a million years?*

The question had been posted over ten hours ago from an unpronounceable place in Canada. There were no replies yet, so Kaela thought it was a good enough reason to stay in the study.

> **Kaela Willoughby:** *Has your play explained why he will survive a million years? If not, have him come back in ten. By then she will be happily married with a few kids and the audience gets both ... A happy ending for her, an adventure for him.*

Kaela thought about her own mammoth task of writing for the newspaper, "Glad I don't have to write a school play."

The computer beeped at her, "Oh, she has already replied. That was fast. She must have super typing skills … Stop talking to yourself Kaela!"

Phoenix White Feather: *I think you should be writing this, not me! Who says writing is a man's world?*

Kaela quickly typed a reply.

Kaela Willoughby: *Just using a girl's initiative!*

Phoenix was faster at typing than Kaela. Her replies were coming through at such a speed it was almost like the two were having a real conversation.

Phoenix White Feather: *You are right. You can't beat girl power. That sort of makes me feel bad that my girl character is staying behind whilst the man gets an adventure. I suppose that is how I feel. Everyone around me is travelling all over the world and I'm stuck on the reservation.*

Kaela Willoughby: *What's a reservation?*

Phoenix White Feather: *A place where all the Natives live.*

Kaela Willoughby: *Natives of Canada? Like Native Americans?*

Phoenix White Feather: *Yes. Surely everyone knows that? Where do you live?*

Kaela Willoughby: *South Africa.*

Phoenix White Feather: *NO WAY!!!!!! I have never spoken to a South African before. That is awesome. So are there lions in your backyards?*

Kaela Willoughby: *Of course not. Are there bears in yours?*

Phoenix White Feather: *Sometimes. Mainly just before winter, when they have to fill their stomachs up for hibernation.*

Kaela Willoughby: *Really? Wow! The wild animals here are in national parks and they can't get out. It's more for their protection than ours. The parks are big though, about the size of Wales. The only semi-wild animal that roams freely is monkeys.*

Phoenix White Feather: *Monkeys? Like the ones that are always in movies and sitting on people's shoulders?*

Kaela Willoughby: *No, those are capuchins. They are from Brazil. Our monkeys are called vervets. They are cute, but really scary – 'specially the males! Sometimes they break into your house and steal your soap!*

Phoenix White Feather: *Soap? The stuff you wash with?*

Kaela Willoughby: *Yeah! Last week, we spotted a trail of banana peels and guessed we must have had monkey company. When I went into the shower, there was a huge bite taken out of the soap bar! It was hilarious.*

Phoenix White Feather: *Poor Monkey is probably burping bubbles. What other crazy things happen there?*

Kaela Willoughby: *We have this giant worm called a shongololo. It is HUGE. Probably about half the size of your arm. These things are mad. They crawl all over the house, ESPECIALLY into* the bathroom where they wait for you to shower, and then drop onto your head.

Phoenix White Feather: *And suddenly I am glad I never leave the rez.*

Kaela Willoughby: *They won't do anything to you. Can't even bite, but they are a bit creepy. Especially when they crawl into your bed at night. We also have to check our shoes for scorpions. And in summer (which is December to March) we have to check inside the toilets before sitting down, because there might be a snake in there.*

Phoenix White Feather: *Forgive me for never visiting you.*

Kaela Willoughby: *It is awesome down here. You can't beat the animals. Have you ever even seen a herd of elephants in the wild?*

Phoenix White Feather: *Nope. Have you ever sat in the mountains and howled to a pack of wolves?*

Kaela Willoughby: *I have never even seen a wolf.*

Phoenix White Feather: *You don't know what you are missing!*

That night, Kaela slept soundly, dreaming of wolves, bears, and elephants. In the morning, she was almost sad to wake up to a boring bedroom instead of snow-capped mountain or a savannah.

❧ Three ❧

"Okay, drop your irons," Kaela yelled.

This was Apley slang for 'take your feet out of your stirrups'. The beginners did as they were told, and suddenly, all chaos broke loose. Until now, the girls had not been using their legs to grip the horses, and had been leaning on their stirrups. They now flopped around in the saddle like rag dolls, threatening to fall beneath the crushing hooves.

Kaela put her hands over her eyes and peeked through slits between her fingers. She had never expected this to happen.

"Halt!" a voice rocketed across the stables. All eight girls stopped their horses with relief.

Bart came walking up to the ring, still in his school uniform.

He walked straight up to Kaela.

"Need a little help?" he asked. He smiled at her, deepening

his dimples, and for a moment she wondered where her knees had gone.

"Yes, I would love some," she sighed, relieved.

Bart took over the class, and Kaela gratefully walked towards the stalls. Her eyes caught a view of the mountain behind the stable. This was the mountain that surrounded Port St. Christopher and blocked the view of the neighbouring city of Durban. Although the mountain was a fully stocked suburb, the houses were all nestled between the ancient trees – some were even built around the trees. Kaela stopped to look at the beautiful view; one of her favourite things about her home was the nature.

Giant's Throne Mountain held a small nature reserve full of hippopotamuses, rhinoceroses, jackals and wildebeests. She sometimes convinced her father to stop working for a few hours to go for a drive through the park. The jackals ran across the roads in death-defying games of chance whilst the hippos snorted in their dams. You learned to avoid the rhino at all cost. Their car had once been charged by a father rhino because they had accidentally got too close to a baby, which they hadn't seen grazing beside the bushes. They only managed to get away by breaking the five mile an hour speed limit. They had then been fined for speeding and endangering the rhino. Kaela's dad hadn't been very pleased.

"Ah, there is no place like home," she said with a smile.

She took one last look at the suburban forest, thought about Phoenix, who was probably howling to a wolf right now, and continued on her trek to the stables. She was almost there when a mother stopped her. Kaela looked closely at this woman's face, trying to place her. Nothing came.

"Hi – Kiera, right?"

"Kaela," she corrected.

"Oh Kaela, of course. Hi, I'm Samantha's mother."

"Hi," Kaela said awkwardly, half-smiling, and not knowing what this woman could possibly want with her.

"Kaela, I know Wendy isn't around for a while, but Bart told me that you're the next best thing …" she began.

All Kaela heard was Bart saying she was the 'best thing' – well, close enough. A small grin crept onto Kaela's lips; she forced herself to concentrate on what this woman was saying.

"… And I know you are very young but Samantha seems to like you, and that is more important than age. So I guess you would be perfect for it," she said.

"Perfect for what?" Kaela asked. She had clearly missed an important part of this conversation whilst lost in her daydream.

Samantha's mother looked irritated at having to repeat herself, "You would be perfect to host a show jumping competition for the beginners. I feel a little competition in Samantha's life would spur her onto excellence, but there are no show jumping competitions for her to enter. I think making one especially for her is the obvious way forward, don't you think?"

"Show jumping competition? But they haven't even jumped yet," Kaela said.

"So put the jumps really low on the ground."

"There is still skill involved," Kaela frowned.

"So teach them," Samantha's mother said firmly, "I was thinking we should have the competition just between the girls in this beginners' class. It'll have to be in about four weeks though; we're going on holiday next month and I would like all the hustle and bustle done and dusted before then. I'll provide the rosettes of course, but I'm going to need you to tell me how many you will need. I can't be expected to do everything on my own."

So why have the stupid competition then? Kaela thought.

She coughed and tried to find a way out of this awkward situation, "I'll have to talk to Bart about this, he is in charge while his mother is away."

"I've already asked Wendy and she's okay with it. I spoke to Bart too. He said that you and Trixie are the perfect people for the job."

Once again, all Kaela heard was Bart suggesting she was 'perfect'.

"So say you will whip the girls into shape by the sixteenth?" Samantha's mother said.

Kaela looked over at Trixie; she was carefully carrying an armful of lunging whips and attempting to open the stable door. She would kill her if she said yes.

Samantha's mother tapped her foot impatiently. Kaela

couldn't think of a good enough excuse to say no.

"Okay," she finally conceded, "We'll whip them into shape."

Maybe.

Probably not.

"Brilliant! Now just tell me what you'll need."

Kaela told Samantha's mother that she needed to sort the details out first.

She would also have to beg Trixie not to beat her with one of those lunging whips.

Trixie cycled into the parking lot and parked her bike out of the way of the cars, and Jeremy. The dogs came to greet her as they always did, she let them sniff her hands and legs for details of her own dogs and then she made her way to the stable. In the beginners' ring, she could see the girls riding without their stirrups, bouncing an awful lot, some of them almost right out of their saddles. Trixie wouldn't be surprised if one of them fell, but then Kaela would never let it get that far.

Behind the riding rings and in the paddock stood Slow-Moe and Quiet Fire.

"Of course, standing as far apart as possible," she muttered through gritted teeth.

She had no idea why the horses weren't friends. With the

amount of time they spent together, wouldn't a friendship be inevitable? Why then, on a day where Trixie was expected to get them both from the field, were they standing on opposite ends of it?

Trixie groaned and went to find a lead line.

Getting Slow-Moe had been easy; he had come when she had whistled. She deposited him in the stall and returned to the field – much to his confusion. Quiet Fire was another story, though. The huge black horse had no interest in leaving the succulent grass. Whenever Trixie stepped forward, he stepped back. Eventually, she angled herself towards the stable so that Quiet Fire, under his own mischief, continued to step closer to the stalls and rings.

"Ha, got you," Trixie said when he had backed up into the fence and there was nowhere else to go.

She clipped the lead line to his halter and walked him back to his stall.

Once there, she led him in and backtracked to the tack room. She grabbed both of the horses' equipment; she slung her arms through the bridles and supported them with her shoulders, while each arm acted as a bar beneath the saddle.

Quiet Fire's saddle was incredibly heavy, and Trixie struggled under the strain. She almost cried from relief when she was able to put it down.

She looked the horse in the eye, which was a good foot above her own line of vision, "I'll be back for you."

He whinnied and shook his mane.

Slow-Moe, as per usual, stood perfectly still as she slipped his halter off and put his bridle on. The bit slid easily into his mouth and she quickly did up all the buckles. Her practised hand threw the saddle onto his back, and pushed it into place. She reached under him and grabbed the girth. With a lot of huffing and puffing, she clipped it into place. After a quick kiss to his velvet nose and a promise that she wouldn't be long, Trixie raced out of the stall and over to Quiet Fire. She led him over to the mounting block outside. He was too mammoth to tack him inside his stall. She clipped him to the post, and stood up on the block to put his saddle on. She struggled to lift it above her head.

"How does Kaela do this every day?"

Eventually the saddle was on, but she had to practically climb under him to get to the girth. She wrestled it into place but didn't trust it to support Kaela's weight as she mounted. She would have to get Kaela to fix it. While Quiet Fire still wore his halter, Trixie then put the bridle on. She unclipped the halter and stood on tiptoe to clasp the buckles.

By the time she was finished, she felt as though she needed a nap. Her arms ached and she'd managed to work up a sweat.

She leaned against Quiet Fire to catch her breath. He had, thankfully, stood very still during this whole fiasco.

She could only hope the lesson wouldn't be as hard as this.

Bart, it turned out, was worse than his mother. Kaela couldn't remember a time she had worked harder in the saddle. The class had been so intense she'd had to wait until the outride to tell Trixie about the show jumping competition.

"What? Teach them to jump in four weeks? Are you mad?" Trixie said.

"It can be done," Russell said, trotting up from behind them on his own grey mare, Vanity Fair.

Kaela smiled at the sound of his voice. Russell had had a crush on Trixie for about two years, something that Trixie had tried to avoid thinking about at all costs. Kaela turned around to smile at him; he took this as a sign to continue talking.

"I mean it's not like there are going to be international judges there or something, just let them jump."

Kaela couldn't help but laugh, Russell was the epitome of a lovesick puppy. He had pushed his horse so close to Trixie's mount, that there was danger of Slow-Moe having a horse's nose up his bum. Trixie pretended not to even notice. It did paint a very funny picture.

Kaela looked closely at Russell: his dark brown hair matched his eyes, which complemented his dark skin. His face was scattered with pimples, but Kaela was convinced these would clear up in time. Although he was only sixteen, he was an excellent horseman and sat confidently in the saddle. He was also sweet and funny, and one of those genuinely kind-hearted people. He was hardly the plague of locusts that Trixie accused him of being.

"You know what? You are right: all we need to do is teach these kids to stay in the saddle when they go over a ten centimetre high jump. The horses will do most of the work anyway," Kaela said. Her voice faltered as she spoke. She had completely forgotten that above everything else she had to do, she still had an article to write.

"What do you say, Trixie?" Russell asked gently.

Kaela thought that to be his problem, Trixie had no space in her life for gentleness. Everyone in her life was too gentle, too scared of her quick replies and scathing frowns. She needed someone to take command; to argue when she was being difficult; to point out her flaws when she refused to see them, but also somebody sweet enough to never mention it again once she understood where she had gone wrong.

"Come on, Trixie-True, what do you say?" Kaela asked with a bit more pushiness than Russell had used.

"Okay, we'll teach these kids to hang on as the horse sails over the enormous jumps," Trixie said without looking around.

Kaela could feel Russell's excitement, it was as though he were the one to be working with Trixie. That gave Kaela an idea.

"Say Russell, would you like to be a judge with Trixie and

me?" Kaela asked in her sickly sweetest voice. Trixie turned to her friend with fire in her eyes, but Kaela refused to take any notice. Russell practically jumped out of the saddle.

"I would love to."

He looked at Trixie, who looked at Kaela.

"Good, then we just need to find two more judges," Kaela said with a laugh.

"I'm going to kill you," Trixie said later, as she walked up to the stall where Kaela was in the midst of untacking Quiet Fire. It was just the two of them, apart from the horses.

"Oh, don't be such a grouch," Kaela said, trying to keep a straight face.

"How could you invite him to be a judge? That means he'll be with us all day."

"Oh Trixie, this isn't about you! This is about those dear sweet beginners who have to compete in four weeks, and they need fair judging. I just went out and found the person most suitable for the job," Kaela said, using that sweet voice for the second time that day.

"Is that how we're going to play it now? Okay, then. You picked a judge, now it's my turn," Trixie said with an equally sweet smile on her face. She turned and walked away.

Kaela did not trust that smile or that small skip in her step, "Where are you going?"

"To find the person most suitable for the job," Trixie said and ran towards the advanced ring. To her horror, she was hurrying towards Bart.

Kaela ran after her, intent on stopping her before she got there – using violence if she must – but Trixie beat her. Kaela only made it in time to hear:

"Sure, I'd love to be a judge."

⤞ Four ⤝

The next day's English class saw the two friends in a glaring war. Kaela knew it wasn't serious. Trixie just had no patience for Shakespeare, and distracting Kaela in her favourite subject probably seemed more interesting than the alternative. They were warned twice that their staring feud should end and they should get back to A Midsummer Night's Dream. Neither took the warnings seriously, both were kept back at lunch to clean the classroom, and both considered it a personal triumph. They had beaten the system. Whilst the rest of the school was outside in the boiling sunshine, Kaela and Trixie were cool and comfortable in the shaded classroom.

"So, what are we going to do for this competition?" Kaela asked.

As she looked down, she noticed that her school uniform was getting a bit short – the blue dress hung about a good way above her knees. This was a problem: the rule in her school was that the dress had to hang *on* the knees. Wasn't her father going to be so pleased when she had to tell him that it was the first week of school, and she already needed a new uniform?

"Well, we need to find one more judge. Then we have to decide what type of jumping competition it should be," Trixie said.

She threw the sponge at the blackboard to clean it; her theory was that the water splashed further if you threw the sponge than if you just wiped with it. Kaela was sweeping at the other end of the classroom, thinking of her first show jumping competition. She had been eight years old, and was entered with a pony named Hopscotch. He was a really fat old thing, and Kaela had struggled to get the girth tight enough. Needless to say, she'd come in last in the horse and rider presentation competition. The judge had put his hand in the stirrup and pushed down; the saddle had landed up underneath Hopscotch instead of above him.

"Hello? Earth to Kaela. Come in, Space Cowgirl. Competition. What kind?"

Kaela brought her attention back to the present and thought about the rules of show jumping.

"We need a horse and rider presentation competition," Kaela said quickly, attempting to forget her own disaster.

Trixie picked up a piece of chalk and wrote the suggestion on the newly cleaned board.

Kaela then remembered that the first timers had to jump

a cross jump to test their form, she had forgotten to put her heels down and was thrown forward on to Hopscotch's neck. She hadn't been placed anywhere. Actually, she had been lucky to have stayed on the pony.

"We need a form jumping competition," Kaela said.

Trixie wrote that on the board too.

"I think we should have two courses, one just a bit longer than the other," Trixie said.

"Sounds good," Kaela answered.

Trixie wrote it down.

Kaela remembered that her first competition had two courses as well: Hopscotch had followed his nose past the third jump, through the course entrance, and to a bunch of carrots that had been left on the table. Kaela had been disqualified.

The next course, although slightly more difficult, had gone better. Hopscotch had behaved the entire time, and Kaela had been awarded a Clear Round ribbon. Although she had won numerous rosettes as well as medals and trophies throughout the years, that first rosette was the only one that was still on display. Despite the fact that it was faded and only getting older, it held a special place in her heart that no new rosette, trophy or medal could replace.

"We need to figure out how many rosettes we need," Kaela said.

"Four competitions with three winners each is twelve rosettes." Trixie said, grinning at Kaela, who seemed to still be working the sum out in her head. "Normal competitions in South Africa have two grand winners. Considering there are only eight of them, I don't think the grand winners are really necessary. So … twelve?" Trixie said, writing it all down. "And I think they should all be blue, so they all feel like winners."

"Let's also have the last two rosettes, we'll decide what to do with them on the day," Kaela said. "You know how show jumping competitions are, something will always happen."

"As long as they're in blue," Trixie said. She rubbed out twelve and wrote fourteen.

"Did you know that in Canada you can howl at wolves?"

"Did you know that in South Africa you can get eaten by a lion?" Trixie said without looking at her.

"Only if you are silly enough to try and pet the thing."

"Well there are plenty of silly people."

That was for sure.

Trixie looked from her notebook to Mrs George and back again. She could have sworn this woman had been saying the same thing over and over for the last five minutes. Every time she said something that Trixie deemed important, she quickly scribbled it down, only to find it had been said and noted already.

Shouldn't a guidance councillor be more organised? Not for the first time in her life, Trixie believed she could be running the joint.

"So I want you to really think – I mean really think about this – because it is a big decision."

Is that the third time she's said that? Trixie thought.

"As you know, you have to choose *only* six subjects. And two of those are already taken with the languages. You have no choice in this matter – only *four* subjects can be chosen."

That's the fourth time, at least.

"Obviously, you need to think about what you want to do with your life. If you want to be a doctor, you have to take a science and biology, if you want to be a pilot you should take geography, and if you want to be an archaeologist you have to take history."

"Honestly, are we just here to waste time?" she eventually whispered to Kaela.

"Probably. How much detention time do you think I will get, if I tell her that an archaeologist is probably better off with geography? They have to know rocks and sand and stuff, so that they don't accidentally kill themselves in landslides. Only historians *have* to know history," she rolled her eyes.

"Well by that logic, we would both be in detention because I so badly want to tell her that a pilot needs maths more than geography."

Once again, Trixie thought she could be running this place.

"So you all need to go home and think about what it is you want to do when you are older."

If only it was that easy.

"Now remember, *only* four subjects. *Four!*"

Trixie sighed, she wanted to take ten subjects just to get on Mrs George's nerves.

She wrote down the list of subjects she wanted:

English
Afrikaans (she didn't actually want that, she wrote it with a sneer.)
Science
Maths
Chemistry
Physics
Computer Science

There was no use, she would simply have to work her brains out with seven subjects instead of six. She couldn't afford to lose one of the science subjects, as she had no idea which direction she would be going within the scientific world.

For all she knew, she would drop chemistry and then want to be a biochemist.

Or drop physics and want to be an astrophysicist.

Or drop computer science and want to go into engineering.

She would have to take all seven. She would have to bow to the inevitable.

"Attention everybody," Tessigan called.

Six faces looked up at the editors.

"As you all know, the first edition of *The Primary Blab* goes out at the end of the month, so we don't have much time to write articles," she began.

She went on to explain what was expected of the journalists and editors. Kaela knew that she had to write an article of substance. The year before she had written about teachers and school events, but as sub-editor, she now had to write about something with a bit more 'importance'. She hadn't quite figured out what that was just yet.

"Kaela, do you know what you are going to write about?" Tessigan asked.

Kaela shook her head. There were so many important things out there that she didn't know where to start looking.

"Well, think about it and get back to me," Tessigan said with an encouraging smile.

"Sure," Kaela nodded, trying to sound convincing, but she wasn't so sure she would be getting back to Tess any time soon.

The competition really had thrown a spanner in the works.

"One friend request," Kaela muttered as she stared at the screen.

She was meant to be researching for her article but

LetsChat had called her name, especially when she saw who had sent the request.

Phoenix White Feather wants to be your friend.
Do you know Phoenix?

Accept   **Decline**

She hit *accept* and then *view profile*.

Phoenix was fifteen years old and in high school. She had three older brothers, and three younger brothers.

"That is a lot of testosterone," Kaela said with big eyes.

From her profile, it looked like Phoenix was more than just a little bit sporty. There were football photos – or 'soccer' as Phoenix knew it –, basketball, tennis, badminton, swimming.

Horse riding.

Kaela clicked on the picture of Phoenix on a beautiful palomino. The caption said: *Wind Whistler and I enjoying the sunrise. Love these moments with my girl.*

Kaela quickly typed: *She is beautiful!*

She wanted to write a comment of essay proportions asking questions and telling Phoenix of her own riding adventures, but decided that scaring this new friend away would not be in her best interest. Instead, she just looked at the picture. Phoenix was bareback with her waist-length hair loose, something Kaela would never have even dreamed of doing. Riding bareback was dangerous enough, doing it with

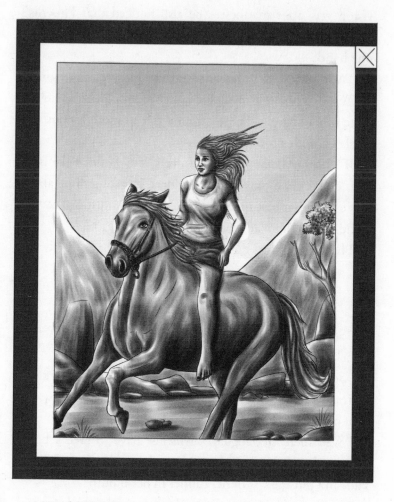

Wind Whistler and I enjoying the sunrise. Love these moments with my girl.

the risk of your hair blowing in your eyes and blocking your vision was utter madness! She also noticed that Phoenix's toes were pointed down and she held the reins with only one hand.

"Wait, seriously?" Kaela asked the picture and zoomed in. Wind Whistler had no bit in her mouth and instead she wore a braided hackamore around her muzzle, "Seriously." Kaela's mouth dropped open.

If Phoenix been at Apley Towers, she would have been considered the most reckless of riders, but something about this easy-going picture told Kaela that this must be the way of riding for the Native Canadians.

Phoenix had just raised the bar to unreachable levels.

"Seven subjects? Are you mad?" Melody asked her sister in disbelief.

"Seven is a lot," their father said. "You know the workload increases. That's why you only pick six, because there is such a lot of work."

"Well then the languages will just have to take a back-burner while I focus on the subjects that truly matter," Trixie said, and put the last of her dinner in her mouth.

She chewed slowly, realising that her mother had not said anything during the meal.

"I can barely cope with six. And I have the creative subjects.

You have the ones with information that never ends."

"Are you insulting the creative subjects?" her father asked in surprise.

"Of course not, machines will replace the artists last. Frankly, the scientists will be the first to be replaced."

"The scientists build the machines," Trixie argued.

"And that is why they go first."

"Your logic is *asinine*."

"Bet you got that word from Kaela – a word artist."

Trixie said nothing.

"Like I said," Melody shrugged and went to continue, but finally their mother spoke.

"Why don't you use your time wisely and spend this year by getting as far ahead of your work as possible? That way, when you have your seven subjects next year, you will have already made a start on the work and understand it. It won't be such a shock to the system."

The family stared at her in surprise.

"I took eight subjects, all maths, accounting and business subjects, so they were no walk in the park. If I could do it with eight, you can do it with seven."

Trixie smiled and nodded, made strong by her mother's belief in her.

"Your horse riding might have to cut back though."

Trixie stopped eating as the rest of the table avoided looking at her.

Suddenly, seven subjects didn't seem like such a good idea.

✿ Five ✿

"You can't expect too much from them at this level, I think you should work on rise and fall for now, then you can move them into a trot. 'Kay?" Bart said.

"Sounds like a plan," Kaela said.

The two stood in the middle of the beginners' ring, Bart still in his school uniform.

Kaela watched as he gripped his tie and began to undo the knot.

It was still hot, the sun glowed orange in the sky, bursting through the scattered clouds and making the pair of them sweat in the heat. A small breeze blew through the oak trees, bringing the scent of the Indian Ocean with it. Everyone paused and sniffed the air, remembering that they were cozy between ocean and mountain, lost in nature and protected by it.

"Are you going to be okay to teach this class?" Bart asked.

"I'm sure I will be. Should the more advanced riders canter in this heat?"

Bart looked up at the sky, and quickly turned away when the sun's glare became too much. He looked at the horses with watery eyes, "It's too hot. I'm dying, and I'm not covered in hair. Well, not horse hair anyway. I'm gonna go get changed. I'll leave you to it."

Kaela watched him leave and then turned to her wards.

"Okay girls, we're going to train you to ride without your stirrups, so drop your irons," Kaela called to them.

She thought of the picture of Phoenix. Had she ever learned to ride with stirrups? Was what she did more free and enjoyable? Kaela could never imagine Phoenix riding in a circle, doing odd exercises to test her balance. Maybe it was better that way – who was she to say the Apley way was the only way?

Kaela taught the beginners how to grip with their calf muscles, and had them push themselves up and down using only their legs, a term called 'rise and fall'. She then took them into a slow trot and had them grip with their legs. They weren't going to win any prizes for form, but at least they were no longer rag dolls.

"Remember, move with the horse. When the horse is going up, don't go down," Kaela said.

Trixie came into the ring, rubbing green goo off of her jodhpurs, "I hate green hay!" she cried to nobody.

Kaela laughed, green hay mixed with horses that

were more than happy to share kisses always made a bad combination. For some reason Trixie was always the one to get their slobbery affection.

"Please build the jumps for the little 'uns for me," Kaela begged, showing Trixie her best attempt at puppy eyes.

Trixie gave the green slobber one more rub, and began building the jumps.

"What are we doing now?" ten-year-old Kirsten asked, staring intensely at Kaela and raising her eyebrows.

Kirsten was the little sister of the stable bully, Bella, and much to everybody's dismay, Kirsten was turning out exactly like her big sister. Kaela had always just ignored her, but at the moment that would be unfair instructing. As much as Kaela hated to admit it, Kirsten was quite a good rider for her age. She was already capable of cantering and making it successfully over the trotting poles. The problem was that she knew it, and just like her sister, she had taken to belittling and tormenting the other riders.

Kaela had spent the last few hours coming up with an inspirational speech for these little ones and come waters high, she was going to say it. She took a deep breath and beckoned the girls in closer to her.

"Well as you know, there are no show jumping competitions for riders of your limited skill. Yvonne, Samantha's mother, has graciously – if not crazily – offered to host one just for the eight of you," Kaela called up to the riders. The majority of them were on ponies, which were not too high up, but the three best riders were all on horses, which towered above her. She had to strain her neck just to look at the little riders.

There was clapping and whispering from the girls, Kaela held up her hands to get silence.

Trixie snorted, "Yes, Queen Kaela," she whispered.

Kaela ignored her, "Trixie and I are going to be organising it, we have decided that it will be as similar to a proper competition as we can get it. We will tell you all about it after class. For now we are just going to teach you to jump."

Kaela had most certainly not anticipated the reaction. Six little girls began shaking their heads, Samantha actually began trembling. But at least the last two sat confidently in their saddles. One was a small girl named Shanaeda, who had mastered the trotting poles weeks ago. The other was Kirsten. Kaela assumed that Kirsten could already jump, it was written all over her smug face.

"Don't worry, the jumps will be low, they are only ten centimetres off the ground," Kaela said to the quivering riders.

"Will we be taking the jumps at a trot or a canter?" Kirsten asked.

At the word 'canter' the other girls' anxiety turned to outright fear. They were affecting the horses, who began stepping backwards and shaking their heads. Kaela frowned and clenched her fists.

"You will be taking this jump at a trot, and relax, if you

don't want to do it you don't have to," Kaela said, glaring at Kirsten and then turning to the other riders comfortingly.

This seemed to do the trick. Kaela was just about to continue when a loud commotion erupted from the other side of the ring.

"OUCH!" Trixie cried.

The riders all turned to look at the injured girl.

"What happened?" Kaela asked, the horses were blocking her view and she imagined Trixie was unlikely to be seriously hurt.

"She was carrying three poles and dropped them on her foot," Rebecca said.

"Is she all right?"

"You stupid pole! You better watch your back from now on!"

"She's okay," Rebecca said, giggling.

"Okay, get those horses warm again, walk on."

When the jump was built, Kaela picked one rider from the bunch and kept the rest walking. Seven-year-old Amy was the youngest rider in the class, the tiniest too. Everyone at Apley was of the belief that Amy was an opposite match of Kaela: where Amy had waist-length blonde hair, Kaela had waist-length mahogany hair. Amy's little face was dominated by her large brown eyes, while Kaela's bright blue eyes were the first thing you spotted on her otherwise colourless face. Amy was quiet and reserved and had to test the waters before she jumped, Kaela was loud and opinionated and believed that testing was for those with too much time. Even so, Amy stayed enchanted with Kaela and everything she did. Kaela thought of Amy as her little 'Apley sister' …

"Okay guys, listen up. You will put your horse into a trot. The horses can see the jump in front of them, so one nudge with the foot will get them straight into a trot. Don't worry, these are old school-horses, they will take care of you. All you have to do is squeeze really hard with your calves and right before the jump, go down like this," Kaela bent forward to show the riders the correct position. All the riders, with the exception of Kirsten, imitated her.

"Good, now the jump is not high at all," in fact the pole was nearly touching the ground, "so the horse will not lift that high up, which means you will not lose your seat, provided that you squeeze with the calves," Kaela said.

Kirsten put one gloved hand in the air, "Can we hold on to the horse's mane when we jump?" she asked.

"No, you may not," Kaela called back.

Kirsten's face fell, Kaela felt like laughing, but knew that wasn't very professional. Wendy wouldn't be very happy if she found out Kaela had been laughing at the beginners.

"Holding the horse's mane when you jump is bad form: it looks tacky and it shows you are not relying on your legs. In this competition, anybody who holds onto the horse's mane will be disqualified," Kaela said.

She remembered how badly she had wanted to hold the horse's mane when she first began jumping, she had not been allowed to either. It was better that riders learnt that from the beginning.

"Okay Amy, are you ready?" Kaela asked.

Her head nodded yes, but her eyes screamed no. Kaela went up to the horse and rider, Amy was riding the stable's only palomino – Caesar. Kaela stroked his golden neck while speaking to Amy.

"Just relax, the more relaxed you are the easier it will be. Remember to grip with your calves," Kaela saw Amy's leg muscles flex as she pushed her calves against Caesar's side. Caesar began walking forward as he was trained to do at sudden pressure from the rider's legs, but Amy halted him quickly. Caesar came to a complete stop, awaiting his next instruction.

"You see, you can control him perfectly, nothing to be afraid of. Now just remember to go down right before the jump. You ready?"

She nodded, looking more confident this time. Kaela got out of Caesar's way and Amy gripped with her calves. Caesar began moving forward, she then nudged him with her heel and he sprang into a trot. She posted well, and went down right before the jump. Caesar's front hooves left the ground; he bent his knees slightly and pushed himself forward with his back legs. He landed with a small thump on the other side of the jump and Amy straightened up, she let him trot for a bit and then brought him back to a walk.

"Hooray, well done Amy!" Trixie cried.

All the riders, spectators and grooms clapped for the first time jumper, whose cheeks turned redder than a tomato.

"Was it that bad?" Kaela called to the blushing girl.

"No, it … it was fun," she said shyly.

"You see how easy that was? Who's next?" Kaela said.

One by one, the riders came to jump and all landed on the other side with no problems. Even Kirsten did well, despite the scowl she pulled at not being able to hold the mane.

When everyone had jumped, Kaela dismissed the class and sent them all on their first unsupervised outride.

"You sure that's a good idea?" Trixie asked.

"The horses will take care of them."

"Are you sounding all mystical for a reason?"

Kaela looked at her friend, "One day you are going to get in real trouble because of your backchat."

"And will you sound all mystical until that day?" Trixie smirked.

When the beginners returned, the grooms took the horses and all eight girls walked over to the table where Trixie and Kaela sat waiting.

"Did you enjoy that?" Trixie asked.

"Yes!" they all yelled.

"Take a seat, we need to talk to you about the competition," Kaela said.

There were five chairs, which the girls filled. The last three girls sat on their friends' laps.

"The competition will take place in four weeks at twelve o'clock. I will be a judge as well as Trixie, Russell, and Bart. You–"

"Wait a minute," Kirsten interrupted, "there have to be five judges, not just four."

"We know that, we are still looking for the fifth one," Trixie said quickly. Kaela threw her a warning glance and Trixie smiled cheekily in return.

"The fifth judge will more than likely be Wendy, but if she is not back by then, we will ask either a groom or an older rider. Is that okay with everybody?" Kaela asked.

Seven tired little faces nodded their approval, Kirsten stared at Trixie.

"The competition will take place like this: first there will be horse and rider presentation. There, you and your horse will be judged on your appearance," Kaela said.

"We expect you all to be in jodhpurs and the official Apley Towers shirt. If you are wearing knee-length boots, we expect them to be shining; if you are wearing chaps, we expect you to wear the correct riding shoes. You will all have your hair neatly tied up, either in a plait or a bun," Trixie instructed.

"And you will all have to wear your hard hats," Kaela added.

"If you need anything else, like crops or gloves, you are welcome to use them," Trixie said.

"We expect you to be neat and well presented," Kaela said.

"Why don't you just tell us to come in a full championship riding outfit? Wouldn't it be easier?" Kirsten said.

"Well, you can come in a championship outfit, but then I'm going to fail you on improper dress," Kaela said indifferently.

"Your horse's tack," Trixie continued, "will be spotless; I want to be able to see my reflection in the stirrups."

"The horse will be fully tacked and we expect you to do it yourselves," Kaela added.

"But we don't know how," Danielle said.

"We were coming to that," Trixie said with a smile. "This Saturday, there will be a class, it's free so we expect you all to be here."

"There is going to be no riding, just come in clothes that can get dirty. We are going to teach you to clean your equipment, groom, and tack the horse," Kaela said.

"What if we already know how to do that? Some of us do have sisters who ride, you know," Kirsten said.

"Well then it is even more important for you to be here, so we can check you've been taught right," Kaela said.

"I don't for a second believe that Bella knows how to clean tack, she has never done it before," Trixie whispered to Kaela, and then turned back to the youngsters. "On Saturday we will teach you everything you need to know about presenting the horse," Trixie said.

"Your next competition will be a form jumping competition. We judge how the horse jumps, and how the rider looks," Kaela said.

"But we've only started jumping, we don't look good," Rebecca said.

"We know, we are only testing you on one jump and we are not going to be strict. We will work on the form jumping tomorrow," Kaela said.

"The last two competitions are going to be the typical course competition. The first course is only four jumps long, while the second course is six jumps and the course itself is a bit more difficult," Trixie said.

"But remember, you only have to do what you want to do, if you don't want to do the last course you don't have to," Kaela added.

"Are there going to be ribbons?" Shanaeda asked. She was practically hidden behind Danielle, all Kaela could see was a pair of little brown eyes poking out.

"Yes, three rosettes for each competition," Trixie said.

The pair had decided not to tell the girls about the last two ribbons.

"That, ladies, is the competition in a nutshell," Trixie said with a smile.

"Can we bring people to watch?" Rebecca asked.

"Of course, bring as many as you want, we are going to have a small party after the show, so the more people there the better," Trixie said.

"All the information we have just told you and a bit more is in these letters, please take them home to your parents," Kaela said.

"We also have permission slips that we need your parents to sign, please bring it to class tomorrow," Trixie added.

Once the letters were given out, as well as the permission slips, the girls went home. Trixie and Kaela stayed at the table and watched the intermediate class trot around the ring. They had had to miss their class for the meeting with the girls. But they didn't mind, Bart told them they could make it up on Saturday after the beginners had left. The girls sat in silence. Trixie watched Bella's form, trying to find the fault in it. Trixie and Bella were old riding enemies, and rivalries ran deep. Trixie was generally better at dressage, but Bella had a better horse – neither of them ever forgot these facts.

Kaela watched Bart, thinking how much he looked like his mother when he taught. Then her attention found its way to the article that she had to write. An empty page sat on her desk. She wouldn't say it was the only thing she was thinking about right now, but the empty page weighed heavily on her mind. She either had to pull her socks up and get the job done or she would risk losing a spot on the writing course. She badly wanted to get on the J. M. Barrie Writing Course. She believed her future lay in the balance.

She was about to get up and go home when she caught sight of the horses in the feeding paddock. They looked so calm, as if they didn't have a care in the world. At that moment, Kaela was incapable of leaving. There was a small voice in the back of her head struggling to make itself heard.

If she was completely still, she could hear it say: *"Writing courses are for adults . You will look back and wish you had spent less time growing up, and more time with the horses"*.

She ignored this voice, she had plenty of time for horses, she needed to hurry up and get her career sorted. Or at least, learn the basics of writing.

Trixie had also found peace in the view of the horses. There were seven in the field.

One for each subject, she thought.

Strangely, Slow-Moe wasn't one of the seven. Was the universe telling her something? Seven subjects in exchange for her time on horseback? Did she really want to make that sacrifice?

Trixie and Kaela didn't speak; each was lost in thought, thinking of the sacrifices they weren't sure they were ready to make.

Phoenix: Hi Kaela,

Thanks for the add. I just looked through your photos, South Africa looks amazing! The photos of that giraffe were unreal. I can't believe she just came up to your camp and dug through your pic-nic basket. That was AMAZING. And the ones of the lions walking past the car. WOW! I showed them to my brothers and mother and they just stared at the screen, gobsmacked. It must be amazing to live there. What were those mountains? They looked cool too.

Kaela quickly clicked *reply* and began typing.

Kaela: Those mountains are the Drakensburg. Or as they are locally known … The Dragon Mountains. It gets really cold there, obviously not as cold as Canada, but far colder than the rest of South Africa. This crazy mist surrounds them most of the time, making it look like dragon's breath. I love going there. We don't go very often though. My father is a homeopath with his own practice, so if he doesn't work, the practice shuts down. So we very rarely go on holidays. Not to mention we live in one of the 'holiday hotspots' of South Africa. So where do you go on holiday when you live on holiday? When we do, it is mainly just a long weekend to a national park or the Drakensburg, which isn't that bad … I miss riding if we are away for too long.

She sent the message, and looked through the rest of her notifications. Phoenix had gone through a lot of her photos and commented, mainly on the animal pictures from her trips to Kruger National Park. Kaela had never lived anywhere else, and had begun to take her home for granted. It took a girl on the other end of the world to remind Kaela how truly blessed she was to grow up with wild animals and experiences that people paid an awful lot of money for.

There was one comment that stood out though.

Phoenix White Feather: *I love your little riding school. I have often wondered what it would be like to have structured riding lessons. Or even to use a saddle. It all looks like something from another world.*

Kaela read the comment out loud.

The picture had been taken a year before, at a jumping show that Apley Towers had held. Kaela had walked away with two blue ribbons and one red. In the picture she stood next to Quiet Fire, grinning like a Cheshire cat and displaying her winnings. The stable, in all its sun-soaked glory, stood behind her, looking like a calm haven that it never was.

Trixie commented on the picture before she could reply.

"Good timing," Kaela quipped, and then read what Trixie had to say.

Trixie King: *Funny that, Kae was saying the exact same thing about your riding. She says it looks like something from another time. I think the two*

of you are cosmic twins (I'm only slightly threat-
ened, she is MY best friend after all).

Kaela was about to reply when Phoenix commented.
"How fast is this woman at typing?" It was unreal.

Phoenix White Feather: *Hello Kaela's best friend. Very nice to meet you. You have nothing to fear from me. How about we be cosmic triplets?*

Trixie King: *You can be the Canadian branch and I'll be the South African branch.*

Kaela Willoughby: *Where does that leave me?*

Phoenix White Feather: *Too slow. Now you take the minutes of the meetings.*

Trixie King: *You should learn to type quicker.*

Kaela Willoughby: *You should be doing homework.*

Trixie King: *So should you AND you also have an article to write. Stop messing about on LetsChat.*

A small blue square popped up on the side of Kaela's screen. She quickly read it.

Phoenix: What does your article have to be about? What is it for?

Kaela: School newspaper. Has to be about something 'important'.

Phoenix: Oh, that narrows it down.

Kaela: Well that's my problem. I can't figure out what to write. They say 'write what you know'. I know horses, that's not really important.

Phoenix: I'm sure that about one hundred million people have just disagreed with you: horse breeders, trainers, riders, probably a cowboy or two.

Kaela: Well none of those people read my school newspaper.

Phoenix: So write about something else that you know. Talk about charities. Charities are HUGE. My grandfather is running for Tribal Chief, and he started his own charity years ago. His entire campaign is centred around this charity.

Kaela: He is running for Chief? Like a real Chief? Like you see in movies?

Phoenix: Yes, he is running for the Chief of our tribe, it's a bit like a mayor. The elections are in a few weeks. So I'm telling you – find a charity, write about it.

Another little box flashed across the left corner of her screen and she clicked on it. It was another notification from Phoenix. A new photo of Kaela's dogs loaded. Her screen filled with two beautiful grey and white Alaskan malamutes with three blue eyes, and one brown one, between the two of them. The caption said: Lakota and Breeze.

Phoenix White Feather: *Lakota? Did you know that Lakota is a Native American tribe?*

Kaela quickly answered:

Kaela Willoughby: *It also means 'friend', right?*

Phoenix White Feather: *Yes, it does. Not in my language though. Friend is KODA!"*

"Koda," Kaela let the word slip off her tongue like a mountain stream on its way to the ocean, "koda, what a beautiful word."

It was a word which would not leave her. Throughout homework, dinner, showering, and getting ready for bed, the word swam through her brain over and over again. It caused so many waves, that she was forced to read a book to silence it.

Peter Pan sat on her nightstand, the place it had occupied since her mother had been around; she had placed it there almost ten years ago.

She opened it on a random page and read the words to herself. She loved *Peter Pan*. She would have probably loved it even if her mother hadn't read it to her every night until the night she disappeared. Maybe this was another reason she was desperate to do the J. M. Barrie Writing Course – J. M. Barrie was the writer of *Peter Pan* and he held a special place in her heart, and her mother's.

Kaela's great-grandfather had bought an original first printing of *Peter and Wendy*, and had taken it to James Barrie himself to sign. The author had written, *'Find Neverland wherever you go'*, followed by his name. That book, surviving the ship to Africa and then life with two unruly male descendants, was now sitting safely inside a glass cabinet in the dining room.

Kaela had taken Mr Barrie's advice. She had found her Neverland at Apley Towers.

Trixie brushed her teeth a bit harder than she needed to. The bathroom she shared with her sister still smelt moist from Melody's shower, but that wasn't what had perturbed her.

Who was this Phoenix White Feather?

At first, when Kaela had mentioned her, Trixie had thought nothing of it. Kaela liked to talk and never ran out of people to talk about. But now, Phoenix was apparently a friend on LetsChat and commenting on everything Kaela had ever put up.

It was only slightly threatening.

Trixie spat the toothpaste, rinsed her mouth and cleaned the sink. She looked around for the hairbrush, couldn't find it, and stomped her way to her sister's room. The hairbrush was always in her sister's room.

"Brush," she said as she entered.

Melody didn't even look up.

Trixie grabbed the brush and pulled it angrily through her hair.

How dare this Phoenix character come in and act like she's known Kaela for years?

"Are you trying to make yourself bald?" Melody asked.

"No, I'm trying to release anger."

"That's why there are stress balls."

She spun and faced her sister, who looked at her in surprise.

"You're wrong. The machines didn't replace the scientists. Another artist did."

With that, she stomped out of the room and went to bed.

❧ Six ❧

"She rode Pumbaa yesterday," Danielle cried.

"That's why I should ride him again today. *And* in the show, because I practised jumping with him yesterday," Kirsten said, quite calmly, staring daggers at the other rider.

"That's not fair, I always ride Pumbaa on a Friday," Danielle said again, her face was turning quite red.

"Well that was before we had a show, rules have changed," Kirsten said.

Kaela could not believe that she had to put up with this, on a Friday of all days; this was Monday moodiness at its best. On top of that, Kaela was not in the best mood herself – suddenly she had a newfound respect for Wendy.

She had tried to write her article before coming to the stables, and had gotten as far as scribbling doodles on the page. She had even tried to research charities but there were so many that she had felt as though she was drowning. Why didn't they all just merge and share administrative costs, leaving more money free for the animals? Wouldn't that make more sense? Why did a fourteen-year-old seem to have more sense than all of the adults put together?

She closed her eyes, took a deep breath, and tried to focus on the good things so that she could get through the day with the demanding beginners.

"Okay, okay, QUIET!" Kaela screamed.

That silenced them both, as well as any talking that had been going on in the stable. Quiet Fire stuck his head out of his stall to see what all the ruckus was about.

"Now, Kirsten is right. The horse you practise on is the horse you are going to ride in the show, so until the show everybody has to stick to the same horse," Kaela said.

"So I'm riding Pumbaa," Kirsten said. Danielle looked as though she was about to burst into tears.

"No, you're not," Kaela said.

It was as though Kirsten had been slapped, the smile fell from her lips and she glared at Kaela.

"Go get the rest of the class and we'll meet at the tables," Kaela said.

She went in search of a groom. Bart wasn't back from school yet, which meant that this crisis had to be handled by Kaela alone.

She rounded the corner and bumped into Joseph, a groom who had worked at Apley Towers since its opening day.

"Joseph, help!"

"What can I help you with, Miss Willoughby?" Joseph said in a sing-song voice.

"The girls are fighting over the horses, and I don't know which one to put with which horse. Do you know who suits who?" she asked.

He only needed a moment to think.

"I believe Caesar is perfect for Amy. Apache is good for Samantha. Give Rhapsody to Rebecca. Star to Shanaeda. Jinx to Jane. I believe Miss Kirsten should have a go at Flight and Danielle can take Sun Dancer," he said. He was tacking Sun Dancer at that moment and gave the horse a good pat on the neck.

"That leaves Michelle with Pumbaa," Kaela said.

"Exactly," Joseph's face erupted in a grin, showing his bright white teeth.

Kaela marvelled at Joseph's genius. He had just solved two problems in one go.

All the beginners wanted Pumbaa. He was the most docile pony in creation; on some days he was bordering on comatose. He was therefore the easiest horse to ride: he did as he was directed with no fuss, he never acted up, and no one was really sure if he could actually gallop. He had a big, round belly and his mission in life was to fill it. As far as the riders could guess, Pumbaa believed that obeying the commands from the little chocolate-smelling thing on his back was just a way to pass the time until his next feeding came. He was, without a doubt, the favourite horse among the younger girls.

Michelle was the most novice beginner of them all. She had only started riding a month ago, but was willing to make up for lost time. So far, she had been riding Sun Dancer, who was getting along in years; she had been an intermediate horse but because of her age had to be bumped down to the less strenuous classes. She was a good horse, and the intermediates were sad to see her go. Unfortunately, Michelle was having a bit of trouble with Sun Dancer. The mare seemed to know that she had an amateur on her back, and took advantage of that. Danielle, though, was extremely firm in what she wanted, and would be able to control the chestnut horse far better than Michelle. By putting Michelle on Pumbaa, Joseph had cooked two meals in one pot.

"You are a genius!"

"That's why the ladies all bring their problems to me."

Kaela laughed, gave him a thank-you hug and raced back to the beginners. She had never heard such complaining and outright petulance as she did when she told the beginners of their new arrangements.

"But I don't like Flight."

"I wanted to ride Flight."

"Sun Dancer is a horse, I want a pony."

"But I ride Jinx."

"Will I actually be able to get Pumbaa to move? Shouldn't a better rider have him?"

"But I want to ride Jinx."

"Until you have your own horses, you will ride who Kaela tells you to ride," Bart said sharply as he walked past. His tone silenced the girls, the look on his face made even Kaela raise her eyebrows.

"Okay, go get your horses and go to the ring," Kaela said quickly.

"Are you okay, Bart?" she called as she jogged behind him.

"Fine, why?"

"You seem a little ... ah ... angry."

Bart shrugged and shook his head, "I'm hot and irritated with friend's mothers having to bring me back home instead of my own mother. And right now I would rather be in the ocean, but instead I have to teach a class in the boiling sun."

He gripped his tie and ripped it off his neck.

"If you want to cancel the intermediate class, I'll spread the news before they all get here. I have everyone's number."

"My mother would kill me. Let me just jump in the pool, try to make some sort of meal from the toothpaste, crackers and cuppa soups that are the only edible food left in the house, and then I'll be back for your class."

"Are you sure?"

"Yes, go, your class is waiting."

Kaela turned back to the grumbling girls who had grumbled all the way to the horses, and grumbled all the way to the ring, grumbled while they mounted, and grumbled as Kaela ordered them to walk on. Five minutes into the lesson, they all had massive grins plastered to their faces. They had apparently been suited with the horse of their dreams.

"Joseph, you're a genius," Kaela said under her breath.

Once again, she had them trot without their stirrups; they were all improving.

Trixie came into the ring and set the cross jump up. The green bars crossed each other at nine inches above the ground, it was a bit higher than what they had jumped the day before but Kaela knew they could handle it.

"Okay everybody, this is a cross jump. It may look high but it isn't," Kaela went to stand at the jump, she put her hand where the poles crossed. "This is where you will be jumping, you have to lead your horse to this cross. If you do not get the horse right in the middle, the horse will not jump. Everybody understand?"

The rest of the lesson was spent on jumping, the girls all had shaky legs by the time the class was over.

"We will see you tomorrow, nine o'clock," Kaela yelled after the riders as they hobbled away.

She had just spotted a familiar blue car in the driveway. It belonged to the father of Bart's best friend. She watched as both father and son climbed out, went to the boot and began unloading brown paper bags. Bart came out to help them take everything into the house.

"At least he doesn't have to eat toothpaste cracker sandwiches for dinner," Kaela said to herself.

Trixie walked up, leading both Slow-Moe and Quiet Fire.

Kaela's hard hat dangled between her fingers.

"Why do you think Wendy is spending so much time in Cape Town?"

Trixie shrugged, "Business stuff I guess. All her family is still in England, so whatever she is doing there can't be personal."

"Poor Bart ran out of food. But Björn's dad just came to drop some stuff off."

Kaela pointed to the car park. Trixie didn't turn around, just raised her eyebrows at her friend.

"Maybe we should keep a close watch on Bart till Wendy comes back," Kaela suggested, "so the poor guy doesn't run out of food or whatever."

Trixie raised one corner of her mouth in a mock smile, "Mmmm-hmmmm. We'll do that."

Kaela came forward and took Quiet Fire's reins, grabbed her hard hat and shoved it on her head, "Thanks for tacking him. Are you ready for the lesson?"

"I'm bringing my skills but who knows if they'll be noticed," Trixie said as she mounted Slow-Moe.

Kaela stopped mid-mount, her stirruped foot holding her up while she stood next to the saddle, balancing in mid-air, "What does that mean?"

Trixie settled into the saddle and smiled.

"What is this, a circus?" a happier Bart asked as he walked up holding a sandwich in one hand and a banana in the other. He pointed at Kaela's balancing act.

"I don't support circuses with animals," she said as she swung her leg over the saddle and settled in.

"Nor do I. Let's do this lesson so I can go jump in the pool and eat," Bart said.

"I agree," Trixie quipped.

Bart span around and looked at her, "Oh, I didn't see you there. Well, come on then."

"Just like I predicted," Trixie said, and nudged Slow-Moe forward.

"What's going on?" Kaela asked as she pulled Quiet Fire alongside.

Trixie smiled at her, "Don't act like you don't know."

"Know what?"

"That the whole world – including the people in it – disappears when fair Kaela and Sir Bartholomew are in the vicinity."

Kaela was spared from having to answer her by Quiet Fire's loud whinny and head-toss.

"Come on girls, it's hot. I want to swim," Bart whined.

"Right-o," Trixie said, grinning at Kaela as she nudged Slow-Moe into a trot.

Bart – who barely managed to spend more than thirty seconds on any other rider but Kaela – made the intermediates jump three-foot jumps without their stirrups.

Both girls fell off and, much to Trixie's dismay, Bella soared over the jumps quite comfortably.

"Phoenix would make mincemeat of her," Kaela muttered reassuringly to Trixie as she brushed the dust off of her Apley t-shirt.

The mention of Phoenix propelled Trixie into excellence – although probably not for the reason Kaela thought.

Her jumping was so well done that Bart congratulated her for thirty-two seconds.

By the time the class was over, the girls hobbled away just as the beginners had done.

"Hey Trixie, did you enjoy your trip?" Bella asked as she led her horse, KaPoe, past the girls.

"Before you judge me, you should probably make sure you're perfect," Trixie shot back.

"Well, actually she did pretty well in that lesson," Kaela said, softly enough for Bella to miss it. She backed away under Trixie's glare.

"Bella," Derrick cried.

All three girls jumped, and Trixie had to bite back her response to Kaela's comment.

"How many times do I have to tell you that it is not Joseph's job, nor the job of any other groom, to care for your horse? In this stable, private horses are groomed by their owners," he said.

Trixie could see Bella was battling not to yell. She relished it all.

"But Derrick, I don't have time, I have other things I have to do," Bella whined.

"Well then you should have thought about that before you bought your own horse – especially a horse that needs as much attention as he needs," Derrick said, he was really battling now, too.

It was rude of Kaela and Trixie to stand watching, but neither made a move to leave.

"He gets exercised," Bella whined even more.

"By somebody who is not paid to exercise him. They are working for free because they feel sorry for KaPoe. Is that how you plan to live the rest of your life, getting your dirty work done by exploiting people?" Derrick's voice was getting louder.

"No, but–"

"I told you not to get a horse, but you went right ahead and did it. Now this is your final warning Bella, if I catch someone else exercising this horse or I see him cribbing in his stall, or if I see that he has gone a few days without being groomed, I will report you to Animal Cruelty and you will be banned from this stable. And as for you two," he said turning to Trixie and Kaela, "don't you have anything better to do than stand here with dirty horses?"

Kaela and Trixie needed no more encouragement; they leapt forward as though they had been stung.

As they always did when they needed to gossip, the girls took the horses into a nursing stall. These were twice the size of an average stall and built especially for new mothers and their babies, meaning more than enough space for two horses.

"How hectic was that?" Kaela said as she began grooming Quiet Fire.

"I'm glad she got yelled at," Trixie said with relish, wishing that she'd had a camera on hand.

"She really did deserve it," Kaela added.

"Of course she did," Trixie said. "She's had it coming for a while."

"Could you put your hatred for the girl aside for once, and think of the horse?" Kaela asked, throwing a soft brush at her friend.

"I am! What she's doing is bad. If she doesn't groom KaPoe, he'll start to get lesions from the rubbing of the saddle blanket, which is probably dirty as well because she never cleans tack – making the problem ten times worse," Trixie said.

"Not only that, didn't you hear Derrick? He said KaPoe was cribbing, and that's really bad. He has so much pent-up energy that in his boredom and agitation, he is chewing off bits of his stall door and eating it. It could turn to colic." Kaela carried on grooming, shaking her head.

Trixie's stomach turned, she had seen only one colic horse in her life but that had been enough. She hoped to never see that horrific sight again.

"And when horses are really bored, they turn to self-mutilation," she said.

"We should report her to Animal Cruelty ourselves, not

wait for her to make one more offence," Kaela said in anger. Horses loved to be groomed when the humans were angry; they pushed that much harder then, hard enough to turn it to a body massage and not just a tickle.

"That's not our call to make. Going behind the owner's back to report abuse could damage the riding school. Anyway, Derrick knows what's going on. He wouldn't let anything bad happen to KaPoe." Trixie said.

"Well it's not fair that she's just going to get away with it," Kaela said.

"Bad guys always get away with everything."

"Not if the good guys stand up to the bad guys," Kaela said.

"You're not in a comic book," Trixie frowned and leant against Slow-Moe.

"I don't need to be. And if you're not going to join me, I'll stand up to the bad guy on my own."

"Well I suggest you try not to cripple Apley Towers while you're at it," Trixie said, and disappeared behind her horse.

"However I deal with Bella it will be in a peaceful way, and Apley Towers will not suffer."

"Do you want to go to 'David's' for supper?" Trixie asked, to change the subject.

'David's' was the Chinese restaurant just up the road from the stables.

"Sure."

"How much money you got on you?" Trixie asked.

Kaela shrugged her shoulders, "Enough."

"Why are you so rich all of a sudden?"

"I washed my dad's car."

"What?"

"You heard me. He says he'll pay me to wash his car once a week."

"Maybe I should ask my dad about that," Trixie said in amazement.

"It's a good arrangement, and I'm also paying my little neighbour a small portion to wash the car for me."

"Well, that's just good business sense."

The girls laughed until the horses put their ears back and began stomping the ground.

"Can you pay tonight, then? I'll pay next time," Trixie asked, smiling her sweetest smile.

"Sure."

Joseph came to take the horses and smiled at the girls, "Embrace what ails you – you can only overcome your enemy with love."

The girls stared at him in confusion, and watched him walk away with their horses.

"What if "what ails you" is a shark?" Kaela asked.

"Then you love them while they are eating you."

She frowned, "Well then I hope there is something I can do before the shark gets close enough to eat me."

Trixie shrugged, "Don't go surfing when sharks are around. That's a good place to start."

The girls made a pit stop at the Willoughbys' house, where they quickly got changed into more restaurant-suitable clothing. While Kaela was in the bathroom, Trixie went through her LetsChat account on her mobile. Russell had taken photos of everyone at the last show jumping competition, and had just posted them on his profile. Phoenix had commented on nearly every photo that had Kaela in it.

Gritting her teeth, Trixie clicked on Phoenix's name and went through her account. She had to stop and stare when she reached photos of Phoenix's older brothers. They were the type of men she imagined when she heard love songs. She wondered if she was allowed to send a friend request to them.

Kaela walked into the room and Trixie guiltily dropped her mobile, awkwardly smiling as she felt her cheeks redden. Kaela didn't seem to notice.

Before leaving, she sent a friend request to Phoenix.

She would embrace what ailed her – and what ailed her's brothers.

As the pair left the house, Kaela caught a glimpse of her empty page. It sat as a reminder of responsibility ignored.

Tess was starting to lose patience with her sub-editor. Kaela needed to write that article, and fast. But for the first time in her life, Kaela had writer's block. She looked at the restaurant on the other end of the road. On any other day, the walk was a short one; on this day, Kaela was willing to bet her riding chaps that the restaurant was actually getting further away.

"I sent a friend request to Phoenix," Trixie admitted. "Have you seen how sporty that woman is? She does, like *everything*. Even rugby. What other girl on earth plays *rugby*?"

"She does have six brothers," Kaela offered. But even she was impressed.

"Yeah, have you seen those brothers? Hel-lo!" Trixie said, and raised her eyebrows with every syllable.

Kaela laughed and imagined two of Phoenix's older brothers. They could be models or actors. They were so good-looking that Kaela's breath had actually caught in her throat when she had seen a picture of them. Apparently Trixie had had the same reaction.

"This must be the first time you and I have ever agreed on the attractiveness of a man," Kaela said.

"It's not my fault that you only like weird guys."

"I don't like *weird* guys. I would just rather choose a man based on his soul, not face."

"That's what boyfriends are for. You choose a boyfriend because he makes you happy. You choose someone to stare at because he makes you drool. Two different situations."

"They are not pieces of meat, Trix."

"Of course not, they'd taste awful."

When the girls eventually arrived at the restaurant, the sun was starting to set. They went in to find a table and were in luck – their favourite table in the corner was open.

"It's my favourite girls!" David cried after Trixie had sat down. "How are you?"

"I'm in the need of a massage," Kaela said.

"I need a maths tutor," Trixie said.

"No, she doesn't. You're head of the class," Kaela looked at her friend with a frown.

Trixie shook her head, "It's not good enough."

"Are you going to have the same tonight, or are you going to try something new?" David asked. He asked it every time they were there.

"The same," both answered.

When David had brought the drinks – cola for Trixie, orange juice for Kaela, as always – the two began discussing the following day.

"Should we start with cleaning the tack, or cleaning the horses?" Kaela asked.

"I think tack first, it's a bigger job, let's get it out the way."

Kaela quickly played the day through her mind – the girls would clean the tack, then go clean the horses, then come back covered in the dirt that used to be on the horses, grab the nice clean tack and put it on the nice clean horses.

That wouldn't work.

"That's not going to work, they're going to dirty the tack when they carry it to the horses. Let's clean the horses first, then the tack, and then tack the horses," Kaela said, counting off the points on her fingers. She ran the new scenario through her head. The girls would clean the horses, go and clean the tack and get themselves clean in the process, and then tack the horses. This way worked better.

"Whatever you say, Captain," Trixie said as David placed their usual order in front of them – sweet and sour chicken for Trixie, vegetable chow mein for Kaela.

Trixie read Phoenix's status with a smile.

PWF: *I've changed my play. The woman is the heroine. She climbs on board the spaceship and travels the galaxy.*

Three boys, who Trixie could only assume were brothers of Phoenix, had commented.

Chiron White Feather: *If she is anything like you, the aliens would kick her off in five minutes.*

Satyr White Feather: *Don't listen to him. Girl power!*

Chiron White Feather: *Is your girlfriend reading this?*

Satyr White Feather: *Probably.*

Arion White Feather: *Why does it have to be a girl/boy thing? Why does the protagonist have to be judged on his/her sex instead of his/her actions?*

Chiron White Feather: *He's going all Tribal Shaman on us again.*

Satyr White Feather: *I agree wholeheartedly, little brother, you are speaking sense.*

Arion White Feather: *Why are you agreeing with me?*

Satyr White Feather: *Because I want to borrow money.*

Chiron White Feather: *You are borrowing money from your little brother? That is just disturbing. You should be ashamed. Phoenix, can I borrow five bucks?*

Phoenix White Feather: *You still owe me five bucks.*

Satyr White Feather: *Borrowing money from your little sister? That is just disturbing!*

Arion White Feather: *Get used to it Phoenix, when you get famous and have millions at your disposal, these two will be begging for money on a daily basis.*

Satyr White Feather: *I disagree completely. When Arion is a famous director with millions at his disposal, Chiron will be living in his basement.*

Chiron White Feather: *That's where I'll bring all my girlfriends. Then eventually my wife and seventeen children.*

Hera White Feather: *Do you lot realise you all live in the same house, and can have an actual conversation instead of typing it on LetsChat?*

Chiron White Feather: *That is so old school, Mama!*

Satyr White Feather: *That just sounds like a lot of work.*

Chiron White Feather: *Oi! Where's my five bucks?*

Trixie's eyes were huge, "Their names are *awesome!*"

Trixie had seen a sculpture of Pegasus at a garage sale once, and been hooked on Ancient Greece ever since. Four siblings and a mother named after Greek stories was enough to have her squirming in her seat.

Kaela quickly clicked on Phoenix's timeline and searched for a picture of her family. She found a snapshot of all seven children as well as their mother, on what must have been a sacred day in the Native Canadian calendar. All eight White Feathers were dressed in beautiful, traditional clothes, complete with feathers and beads. The three older brothers had decorative paint across their faces and naked chests. All family members had their hair in two long plaits that all came down to their waists. Black, white, and red feathers were plaited into their raven hair.

The caption said: *National Aboriginal Day, 21st June. Chiron, Satyr, Arion, Griffin, Ares, Ladon, Mom and me in traditional wear.*

Someone had commented, "*What a beautiful family. True kodas.*"

"True what?" Trixie asked.

"Kodas. Friends."

"They *all* have Greek mythological names. All of them. How unbelievably awesome is that?" Trixie said.

"How awesome are the clothes? And the paint. How amazing is it that their culture and traditions have survived despite colonisation?"

"It's great." With a full stomach, clean skin, and view of the brothers, Trixie was feeling more charitable towards the White Feathers, "They seem to be wonderful people. The brothers are funny. And gorgeous." Trixie grinned.

"Yeah, it looks like a great family."

"I wonder where her father is, though."

❧ Seven ❧

"Press as hard as you can," Kaela said.

The girls had tied their horses along the fence of the beginners' ring, facing into the ring, while Trixie and Kaela had their horses inside as if on display.

"Horses love it when you press hard, so don't hold any strength back," Trixie said, running the brush along Slow-Moe's side.

All eight girls copied her. They were doing a good job today: none were fighting, nor arguing with the older girls, they were doing as they were told. It made the job a lot easier for Kaela and Trixie, and they even started to enjoy themselves.

Once the coats, faces, and ears had been groomed, Kaela taught the girls to clean the hooves.

"First you have to get the hoof off the ground, does anyone know how to do that?" Kaela asked.

Kirsten's hand shot straight into the air. The other girls frowned and groaned.

She had known the answer to every question that day. It irritated Kaela that Bella had actually done a good job of teaching her little sister the basics, when Bella herself seemed to ignore the rules most of the time.

"Yes, Kirsten?" Kaela said.

"You have to run your hand down the horse's leg first, then wrap your hand around the hoof and gently tug. The horse will lift his hoof," Kirsten said.

"Good, okay–"

"What does it mean if the horse doesn't lift his hoof?" Trixie interrupted.

Kaela knew that Trixie was annoyed, and when she was annoyed she took every advantage to throw a spanner in the works. Apparently Bella's knowledge bugged Trixie too.

"It means he's not properly trained," Danielle called out.

Kaela had to laugh: Danielle had unknowingly just destroyed so much tension.

"Yes, it could mean that. But what if the horse is properly trained?" Kaela asked, still laughing.

Once again, Kirsten put her hand up.

"Yes, Kirsten?"

"If he doesn't lift his foot, you are probably being too rough with him: you have to tug *gently*."

"Yes, because one tonne horses are actually quite sensitive," Danielle cried.

This time everyone laughed, including Trixie.

"That's right Danielle, horses are very sensitive. So remember to be gentle," Kaela said. "They are really quite in tune with us humans."

"So watch and learn," Trixie called.

Kaela stood with her back to her audience; she placed her left hand on Quiet Fire's shoulder and ran her hand down the length of his leg. When she got to his hoof, she adjusted her position and wrapped her hand around the front of his hoof. She gave a gentle tug at the hoof, and Quiet Fire lifted it.

"Okay, it's as easy as that," Kaela said, straightening up.

Unfortunately it was not as easy as that: only Kirsten and Samantha were able to do it on their first try. Little girls have very little patience, and after two failed attempts at being gentle, they resorted to pulling the horses' hooves. Not one pony was willing to budge. Eventually Michelle was able to get Pumbaa to lift his hoof, but this had more to do with Pumbaa's ability to assess the situation than having to do with Michelle's skill. After Pumbaa did the kind courtesy of lifting his hoof despite the improper proposal, the rest of the ponies and horses followed. Finally, after a good ten minutes of huffing and puffing, all ten front left hooves were off the ground.

"Now, see all the junk lying against the foot? Just scratch it away with the hoof pick, like this," Kaela scratched at the mud and other bits that Quiet Fire had collected. When she saw the fleshy V where his hoof began, she stopped, "Once you can see a V, stop scratching because that is flesh. If you want a tonne of sensitive animal to trample you, by all means scratch at their flesh."

"Does anybody know what the fleshy V is called?" Trixie said. She was still scratching at Slow-Moe's dirt.

"A frog," Kirsten and Shanaeda said at the same time.

"Very good," Kaela said, moving over to Quiet Fire's right hoof.

"Why is it called a frog? It doesn't look like a frog." Amy said as she inspected Caesar's hoof with a frown.

"Well," Kaela said, hopping excitedly on her toes. "In the horse world, frogs' bones were once meant to symbolise luck. The bone is v-shaped like Caesar's foot, so they named it after the bones."

"Did you read about that just in case someone asked?" Trixie whispered.

"Of course not. I already knew," Kaela rolled her eyes.

"So you just know random things for no apparent reason?" Trixie asked with a mischievous grin.

"One day, one day," Kaela said with squared eyes, "someone is going to beat you with a crop for your cheek."

"And will you know random things for no apparent reason until that day?"

Kaela sighed (so that she wouldn't laugh) and went to check all of the beginners were doing the job right, and doing it gently.

Once all the girls had scratched away the dirt to reveal the proper hoof, Kaela showed them how to scratch away anything that had collected between the hoof and the shoe.

"Remember, gently and slowly," Trixie said.

The grooms picked the horses' hooves every day, so it was highly unlikely the girls would find anything, but Trixie and Kaela had decided the beginners should learn everything they needed to know.

When grooming was complete, the horses were led back to their stables. Everybody then met in the tack room.

"Now remember, cleaning tack is long and boring work."

"Thank you, Trixie," Kaela said.

"Hey, I'm just telling them the truth," Trixie said with a mischievous grin.

Kaela remembered the first time the two of them had ever cleaned tack. They had carted everything out to the feeding paddock, and sat working in the shade. Kaela turned to Trixie. From the look on her face it was clear that they had both had the exact same idea.

"Grab whatever your horse owns, and follow me," Trixie said.

Ten minutes later, nine girls sat on the hill in the feeding paddock, rubbing saddle soap into every nook and cranny. Kaela had gone in search of a bucket and salt.

Midway through her expedition, she ran into Bart mucking out stalls.

"Hi," he said to her as she walked past his stall.

She whirled around so fast she nearly lost her balance.

"Hi," she said breathlessly. She watched him throw the contents of his shovel into the bucket; she thought that mucking the stall had never looked so good.

"Sorry about yesterday, I was annoyed. Didn't mean to take it out on Apley riders."

Kaela waved her hand in dismissal, "Don't worry about it. Your meltdowns are fairly calm – you should see what happens when I lose it."

"Yes, boots take themselves off your feet and fly across the paddock," Bart said with a smile and went back to mucking.

Kaela smiled and nodded, then turned serious, "Are you ..."

"Am I?"

"Are you all right? I saw a food delivery, so I'm assuming you are not eating toothpaste. But are you all right with everything else? You don't need anything?"

"I'm fine. Mum is sorting my life and her stable from a thousand miles away in the west."

"Why is she there, and for so long?"

Bart shrugged, "My dad is up to nonsense, as per usual. She won't tell me anything, but I'm assuming they're fighting over money ... Again."

"Why is he here? I thought he lived in England."

"He does, but he has a company in Cape Town," Bart stopped and looked at her. "My guess is that the company is failing, and Dad is trying to swindle money out of Mum."

Kaela didn't know what to say. She couldn't figure out what was worse: his parents fighting in a war created by money, or his parents not fighting about him. As far as Kaela could tell, Bart only saw his father once a year and he had to fly to England for that. His father had never come down to South Africa for him, yet the man flies down for his company? That had to hurt.

"You guys still in the middle of your lesson?"

"Yes, we're cleaning tack," she said, grateful for the change of subject.

"So, why are you wandering around?"

"Looking for salt for the bits."

"In the feeding room," he said, without looking up.

"Thanks."

Kaela walked away but then backtracked, "Need any help?"

"Nope," Bart said as he finished up and walked out of the stall, "all done for the morning. The only thing left to do is teach you guys. Sorry, girls."

"Is it going to be an easy lesson?"

Bart leaned against the pitchfork with an air of wistfulness on his face, "That depends."

"On what?" Kaela asked with a barely concealed smile. She was loving this game.

"On whether I have a good swim or not."

"Oh you poor thing. While we are slaving away in the sun, you are relaxing in the pool."

"It's a tough job, but someone has to do it," he grinned at her.

"One day, I'm going to get so hot and bothered that I am just going to storm right over and jump in your pool."

Bart looked at her with demons dancing in his eyes, "I look forward to that day."

He rested the pitchfork against the wall, grabbed the wheelbarrow handles and began to walk away, "You better do it before summer ends," he called back to her.

Kaela watched him walk off, the English rose in the African savannah.

Fifteen minutes later, Kaela joined the group with a bucket of salt water.

"What's that for?" Kirsten asked. This time she was genuinely interested.

"What do you think it's for?" Trixie asked.

"I don't know, Bella has never used salt water to clean her tack."

"Bella cleans her own tack?" Trixie asked with fake surprise, or perhaps it was real.

Kaela jumped in before the conversation went any further.

"There are numbers and letters engraved into the bits, find yours and remember it," Kaela said to the group. She waited for them to locate it, "You're going to take off the bits, clean them under the tap over there, come back and soak them in the salt water, then you are going to take them out and clean them again. And the only way you are going to remember which bit is yours, is by the numbers and letters. So *don't forget them*." Eight little heads nodded in unison.

"What does the salt water do?" Shanaeda asked.

"It works as a disinfectant," Trixie said. "It gets rid of any dirt and germs from the bit."

She showed the girls how to take off the bits, and they all went on their way to the tap to clean them.

It was a hot day, and it probably felt hotter because they were doing such tedious work. Kaela sighed and wiped the sweat from her neck.

"One day I'm abandoning everything, and jumping into Bart's pool."

"One day I'm abandoning everything, flying to Canada, and introducing myself to Satyr White Feather." Trixie said as she scrubbed the stirrups, grinning.

When the little girls came back, they dropped the bits into the bucket and set to work cleaning the bridle, reins, and false martingale. When that was done, they retraced their steps back to the tap to clean the stirrups. By this time, the girls themselves were fairly clean too.

Kaela remembered the first time her own beginners' class had to wash bits: it had been a catastrophe. Nine little girls trying to find their bits, all at once, was nothing more than a jumble of fingers and dropped bits and the chaos of sloshing salt water. She had come up with a better way to do it.

"When I call your bit's number, come forward and collect it: SB826," Kaela said.

Jane came forward, took her bit and walked back to the tap.

"MK827."

Next came Samantha, it continued like this until all the girls had their bits and were at the tap.

"Maybe one day I should just wear my swimming costume under my riding outfit, sneak away and jump."

"I wonder how much a plane ticket to Canada costs?"

Kaela thought about telling Trixie what Bart had told her about his father. She decided that maybe it was a moment made just for them, and not gossip to be spread around the stable. She had only a second to feel guilty about keeping information from Trixie before Danielle came up the hill. She was the first person to come back with a clean bit.

"It's clean, how do you put it back on?" she asked.

Trixie and Kaela smiled at each other; this was the moment they had been waiting for. The two had talked late into the night about this one moment.

"Are you sure it's clean?" Trixie asked.

"Yes, I just cleaned it," Danielle answered.

"Are you sure?" Trixie asked again.

"Yes," Danielle said. She looked as though she was starting to doubt herself.

"Then put it in your mouth," Kaela said.

"What?" Danielle practically screamed.

"If you are sure that it is clean, put it in your mouth," Trixie said.

"No way!" Danielle cried.

"Then it's not clean," Kaela said.

"It is clean," Danielle argued. Her cheeks reddened.

"Then what's the problem?" Kaela asked.

"If it is clean, then you shouldn't mind putting it your mouth. I mean, you've cleaned it. It's like it's brand new now," Trixie added.

"But I don't want to put it in my mouth," Danielle said.

"Why?" the older girls asked in unison.

"Because … just because," Danielle said.

"Then you had better go back and clean it until you are comfortable enough to put it in your mouth," Kaela said, and rested a reassuring hand on Danielle's shoulder. She seemed close to tears.

"Ohhhh-kay," Danielle said, and walked away with her head down.

Eight little girls walked up the hill with clean bits, eight little girls walked down the hill to clean their bits again.

Kaela and Trixie laughed until tears ran down their cheeks. The exact same thing had been done to them, and they'd also had to do the walk back down the hill. It was the best way to ensure that the bit was as clean as it could get. To this day Trixie and Kaela cleaned their bits in that fashion, if they were not comfortable enough to put it in their own mouths, it was not clean enough. Trixie's mother had not been too impressed with that way of thinking. She believed her youngest daughter would end up with Mad Cow Disease, but not even she could deny that the salt water was a disinfectant and if anything dangerous had existed on the bit, the salt did a good job of killing it. After four years of having a bit in her daughter's mouth once a week, she finally gave up and accepted that for horse people, stuff like that was the everyday norm.

Rebecca was the first to come back up. Much to the girls' surprise, she came up the hill with the bit in her mouth.

"Tathtth lak methal," she said.

"Well done Becca," Kaela laughed. Both girls clapped for her.

While Trixie was showing Rebecca how to put the bit back, Jane and Michelle came up together. The two had been inseparable the whole day. Kaela assumed that four years from now, Jane and Michelle would be standing on the hill waiting for the new beginners to put bits in their mouths, just as two girls had stood on the hill when Trixie and Kaela had put the tack in their mouths for the first time. It was strange, Kaela thought, the way that such precious information was passed down through the generations.

"Okay, let's see," Kaela said to Jane and Michelle.

The pair put the bits in their mouths for a split second and spat them back out. It was still considered good enough. They received the same congratulations that Rebecca had.

After all eight girls had done the task, the group made their way back to the stables.

The horses were tied to the same place on the fence, and the girls were taught how to tack their mounts.

By the end of the lesson, Kaela and Trixie were so exhausted they weren't sure if they would be able to stay on the horses in their own lesson.

"Trix, I can't get my leg over."

Kaela was once again balancing on only one stirrup, attempting to pull her tired leg up and over Quiet Fire.

"What is with you and the circus acts?" Bart asked as he walked up.

"She can't get her leg over the saddle," Trixie said conveniently.

Bart spun around and looked at her, "Oh, are you having a lesson today as well?"

"Yes!" Trixie cried in exasperation.

"Well," he reached up and pushed Kaela's leg up, "let's get this lesson started so I can jump in the pool."

"Do you ever do anything else?" Kaela asked as she adjusted her stirrups.

"Teach," he raised his eyebrows at her, then sauntered off into the ring.

The two followed him into the advanced ring, where he had them trot in a close circle around him.

Kaela had always found this task most difficult. The inside rein had to be held shorter than the outside rein, and her outside leg had to be placed behind the girth, while her inside leg was directly on the girth. All the while she had to post, grip, keep her back straight, keep her heels down, keep her head, shoulders, hips and heels in line, and keep the horse at the speed she needed him as well as direct him to where he needed to go. It was exhausting and confusing. She could tell you word for word what she should be doing, but actually doing it was hard.

If she concentrated on keeping her outside leg behind the girth, her heel went up and she lost her alignment; but if she concentrated on her alignment, her leg didn't stay behind the girth. Wendy kept saying that it would become natural with practice. So far it hadn't. Trixie, on the other hand, looked as though she could do all of this and still cook a seven course meal on top of that. Kaela tried to look as though she wasn't struggling, but it was easier said than done. She kept taking quick glances at Bart – he had a small smile on his face.

"Just relax Kaela, you're too stiff, move with the horse," Bart said.

Kaela relaxed her muscles a little, Quiet Fire relaxed beneath her. It did not help her riding, but Quiet Fire was more obedient when he was relaxed.

"Now go the other way," Bart instructed.

Trixie slackened her grip on her inside rein and pulled on the outside rein, Slow-Moe turned one hundred and eighty degrees as though he was dancing. Trixie then moved her right leg backwards and hooked her calf muscle behind the girth. She made it look like something from a ballet

performance. Kaela tried to do the same, but lost her seating when Quiet Fire began trotting before she could reposition her legs. She had to grab the pommel to keep from falling.

"Great job guys," Bart said five minutes later.

The girls brought their horses to a stop, and looked at him.

"How about a nice gallop across the feeding paddock?" Bart asked.

Kaela had never heard of a nicer proposition. The girls trotted the horses over to the gate and waited for Bart to open it.

"Yah!" Trixie cried, and kicked. Slow-Moe sprang forward.

Kaela wanted a bit more time, she needed to reconnect with her mount after such a bad lesson. She ran her hand up and down his neck and leant forward to whisper sweet nothings in his ear.

"Aren't you going to gallop?" Bart asked her.

"I'm just reminding him that he will always be my number one boy," Kaela said.

"Does that mean there's no space for other boys?" he asked.

Kaela smiled at him, tightened her grip with her calves, and kicked Quiet Fire into action. He leapt forward without a second invitation.

Quiet Fire was born to run; there was nothing he liked to do more. Kaela buried herself further into the saddle, got a good grip with her legs, pushed her heels down and enjoyed the ride. She forgot about legs behind girths and ballerina dancing on horseback, she forgot about the blank page that

sat on her desk, she just got into Quiet Fire's groove and
rode the back of the wind.

Trixie dried the plate and put it back in the cupboard.
She barely had the energy to do that.

"Have you decided on your subjects?" her mother asked
as she walked into the room.

Trixie shook her head. Truth be told, she hadn't really
thought about it since the arrival of Phoenix in their lives.

"Why are you wanting to take everything?"

"Because I don't know which scientific field I want to
work in. I want to have them all so I have options."

"You will always have options. What you won't always
have is time to ride."

Trixie looked at her mother in confusion, "Time to ride?"

"Yes, do you honestly think that when you are working
as a biochemist in some non-animal testing lab in Italy, you
will have the time to jump on a horse and ride?"

"No, but …"

"These are the last few years where you are free to ride.
You have your entire life to study science. In four years
you will be in university, and that's when you will really be
making all your decisions."

"But, what about getting ahead like you said?"

Sabrina King shrugged, "Maybe I was wrong. I don't

regret all that I didn't study in my childhood, I do regret not taking as much time as I could to just relax and be free."

"But you were brilliant. Ahead of your class."

"And you are brilliant, top of your class. But that is not the only thing life is about. Do yourself a favour and give yourself a break. You can be serious later. You can weigh up chemistry or astrophysics in University. Right now, have fun being free."

❧ Eight ❧

The next few days flew by. Wendy had not returned from Cape Town yet, so Kaela was still in charge of the beginners. To improve the strength in their legs, she kept their lessons stirrup-less. Although they complained (and did they complain), they were improving.

Kaela, herself, was working to improve too. She took an extra five minutes after class every day to practise impulsion control. But even with the extra practice, she had little, if any, improvement.

"You can't improve in five minutes," Trixie said as they mucked out stables one Saturday afternoon.

"I know that and I'm not expecting to. I'm just saying that I should be able to see some improvements by now."

"After only a week?"

Kaela bit her tongue. She didn't want to start a fight with Trixie. But the heat, the stress, and the callous retorts were pushing her buttons. And not in a good way. She shoved the pitchfork into the wheelbarrow, and scooped fresh hay out and into the clean stall.

"Why do you care if you are good at horse riding or not? You want to be a writer. It's not like you have to be the best rider in the world to be a writer."

"I still want to ride well to enjoy it."

"But you're not enjoying it right now."

"Because I'm not riding well."

"That's not how it works. If you enjoy riding, what does it matter if you are good or not? As long as you are having fun. It's not like you are going to have a career in riding."

Kaela didn't want to tell her that since the rejection from the writing course, she had actually been thinking about what she would do if she didn't write. Riding was, of course, at the top of the list.

But for that to be a reality, she would have to be at the top of her game for riding. And right now, she most certainly was not.

That thought sent her backwards … She had a writing rejection and she wasn't the best at riding.

What was she good at then?

The girls worked in silence, both struggling in the heat.

Finally, Kaela said, "Every journalist working on the paper has already handed their article in and they have already been edited. The paper is good to go. The only thing that's missing is the front page, which they have stupidly entrusted me with."

"I thought you volunteered."

"And they stupidly let me. I had no clue what I was getting myself into."

"So just write the article. When have you ever struggled to write?"

"I'm struggling now!"

"Write about the heat and how killer it is."

"And how boring it is."

"I'm just trying to help."

Kaela knew that. But she also knew that Trixie was downplaying her problems and making them less than they were. That irritated her more than anything else.

"It's unfair to make someone so young write about something serious," Kaela said angrily, "Half of the stuff out there I don't even understand."

"What's Tess writing on?"

"How important Shakespeare is in the twenty-first century, and how symbolism can be made between his fictional governments and our real governments."

"Wow," Trixie said.

"Exactly. How am I supposed to compete with that?"

"Why are you competing? You work for the same paper."

"Because, Trixie, I need my article to stick out. If it doesn't, what is the point of it?"

"Um, to write for the enjoyment of writing."

Kaela frowned and stopped for a moment. Trixie was purposefully blocking her.

The idea of Trixie telling her she should be writing for enjoyment was too much for Kaela. She did once enjoy writing, but with so much pressure put on her from the newspaper and her application for the J.M. Barrie Writing Course, writing was akin to dental surgery without a painkiller.

"There is no enjoyment in writing until I am accepted by J.M. Barrie for the course. Until then, writing is work."

"Oh that school!" Trixie cried, "Do you honestly think that going to that school will make any difference to your writing career? Do you think people are going to look at your book and say, 'Oh the writing is rubbish, but look at the school she went to, we should publish her just based on that'?"

"They are going to teach writing."

"You can't teach talent."

"You can hone it."

"And that's what you want? Somebody else to tell you what to do?"

Kaela scrunched her hands in anger, "Why are you being so difficult?"

"I'm being difficult? Me? Are you nuts? You're the one that agreed to teach the little ones, and agreed to be an editor, and agreed to do this stupid show all in the same week." Trixie threw her arms up in the air. "You didn't even ask me!"

"It's not like you are teaching or fretting over the show, so what are you complaining about?"

"No, I'm not teaching. But when you are, I'm running

around tacking up your horse, looking for *your* hard hat, making sure everything *you* need for the lesson is ready for *you*. And I'm also fretting about this ridiculous show. You know, we don't even have everything we need. Where are people going to sit, Kaela? The seven chairs facing the rings?"

Suddenly Kaela remembered that she was the one who was meant be arranging the extra chairs. This thought only made her angrier.

"You know I am going through a crisis too," Trixie continued, "it's not only you. I literally have to choose between school and riding right now."

"No, you don't. You want to get ahead of your year for some unknown reason, and you want to take subjects that you don't even need. It's all your choice, you are not the victim here."

"I'm not choosing subjects I don't need."

"Computer science? Really? What are you going to do with that?"

"Engineering."

"When have you ever wanted to be an engineer? Since you were seven years old, you have wanted to see the stars and study space."

Trixie reeled backwards, "What? No. That is just *one* of the options."

"It was the only option until you saw that subject list. Then suddenly you didn't know what field to go into. Don't you remember that trip to the planetarium where you kept correcting the tour guide? *You* are the reason the school is no

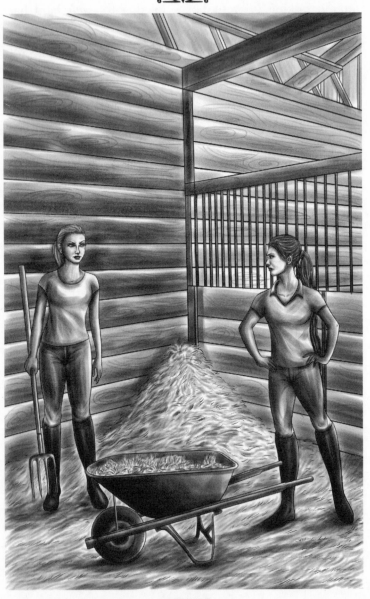

longer allowed to go there for field trips. They didn't enjoy being shown up by a nine-year-old."

"Just because I knew more, doesn't mean that is the field I want. And anyway, I am not the only one who is making myself the victim of my own choices. You take on so much without even consulting me, and I'm just supposed to be dragged along behind you and listen when you complain."

"If you don't want to do it, then don't."

"Fine, I won't," Trixie said.

She threw her pitchfork down and walked out of the stall.

Kaela angrily finished the job and put the wheelbarrow back where it belonged. She could see Trixie cleaning tack at the tables. From the way she was scrubbing, Kaela could see that she was just as angry.

It was all too much for her and she stomped away.

"Miss Willoughby, how are we today?" Joseph asked from inside a stall.

"Been better."

"There appears to be a dark cloud over your head."

"Call that dark cloud Trixie."

"I heard the argument."

"Sorry about that."

Joseph patted the new hay down with quiet contemplation, "You know, I have always found that your friends speak the truth you don't want to deal with." He smiled at her, grabbed the handles of the wheelbarrow and walked off, whistling a tune.

"Whatever," Kaela said under her breath.

Although, there was a voice niggling in the back of her head, agreeing with Joseph. Maybe he was right.

Trixie scrubbed the tack until it shone. Her arm began to ache but she ignored it.

Kaela was crazy. Her writer's brain was inventing mad scenarios where Trixie had been advertising her want of a career in astrophysics since her first year in primary school.

Utter madness.

She squeezed more saddle soap onto her sponge and attacked the stirrup leathers.

"I think it's clean enough now," Bart said as he sat down.

This just made Trixie more angry.

"What do I want to be when I grow up?" she yelled, without thinking.

Bart shrugged, "Something about stars isn't it?"

Trixie's eyes widened, "I have never said anything about wanting to be an astrophysicist. I have just said that I am going to go into science."

Bart shrugged again, "You don't need to tell anyone. We can tell. When someone mentions stars or planets, you start lecturing us about them. Don't you remember there was that one rider who told us that Mercury completed a revolution in the same amount of time as Earth? You lectured that guy

"That's for the grooms to do, not the riders," Bella said without looking up.

She was right, only the grooms were allowed to clip coats, manes and tails, but it was the rider's job to bring it to their attention. It was so typical of Bella to assume that she needn't concern herself with that sort of stuff.

Kaela shook her head in irritation, and then it hit her.

It hit her like a stampede of Apley horses galloping downhill in a lighting storm. She had an idea for the article *and* a way to teach Bella a lesson. She had caught two butterflies in one net.

"I've got it! I've got it!" Kaela cried and ran out of the stables, leaving riders and horses to stare after her.

She ran all the way home, through her garden, through the house, and into her room. She threw herself at the desk, picked up her pen and put it to paper. In less than half an hour she had an article. As soon as it was finished, and she'd read through it to check it made sense, she phoned Tess.

"I've written it. It's done. It's here."

"Great," Tess sighed as though the world had just been lifted off her shoulders, "what is it?"

"It's an article on how important it is to take care of your animals. But it is sort of the opposite of how the articles are usually written. It's about what *not* to do."

"What not to do?"

"Yes, I've used ideas that Bella has given me. But I don't mention her."

"She'll probably still know it's her you are talking about."

"Probably, but maybe that will wake her up a bit."

Tess was quiet for a while. Kaela knew that she would think it was a good idea; Tess was an animal lover too.

"I actually think that's a good idea," she said finally, "it's an article that gives good advice, and it shows that there are bad guys that live amongst us and they need to get their act together."

"That's what I was aiming for. I've also included information about a local animal charity. It started out being just for dogs and cats, but they've started taking on horses as well and they're struggling with the costs. So I have put their donation details in the article."

"Brilliant idea. Charities are always winners."

"So I have heard."

"Do you have a photo of you and your horse?"

"Why?" Kaela asked.

"Front page needs a photo," Tess explained.

Kaela looked down at the photo frame on her desk. It was a picture of Trixie and herself standing on either side of Quiet Fire. It was a close-up of three happy faces.

"Yeah, I've got one."

"Then we'll use that one. This is a good idea Kaela, well done."

Kaela quickly typed a status and hit enter.

KW: *I've finally finished the article. Only took three weeks, four meltdowns, five gallons of ice cream, six bars of chocolate and seven other foods that would give my health-crazy dad a heart attack if he knew I'd eaten them (joking, by the way).*

Within a few minutes, ten friends had liked the status and commented their congratulations. Kaela was not the least bit surprised when a little blue box popped up on the side of the screen.

Phoenix: Congrats.

Kaela: Thank you. Glad to have it out the way.

Phoenix: Is it hard to live with a health-crazy father?

Kaela: My dad is a homeopath, so it's normal for me now. I don't want to eat rubbish, and aside from the odd Chinese meal, I don't really.

Phoenix: What's a homeopath?

Kaela: He uses natural foods and medicines to

treat people the way that doctors do. Veganism and healthy living is all I've ever known.

Phoenix: Wow. My hat is off to you both. My family have always eaten really badly, we've tried to sort it out in the past few years, but it's not easy. Especially when vegetables are so expensive and junk food is so cheap.

Kaela: Can't you grow your own vegetables?

Phoenix: We're trying.

Kaela: In Africa, things grow so easily it's actually scary. I have accidentally grown an apple tree and an entire tomato farm.

Phoenix: Accidentally?

Kaela: Yeah, I threw the apple core on the ground. A year later there was a tree. And we have a compost bin at the bottom of our garden, one night I was too lazy to walk down there, so I threw the tomatoes into the garden thinking the birds would eat them. A few months later there were tomato trees everywhere you looked.

Phoenix: Does it attract the monkeys?

Kaela: Thankfully no. It does attract bushbabies, which I love.

Phoenix: What's a bushbaby?

Kaela: It is a tiny little fluff-ball of a cuddly animal with huge eyes. It honestly looks like a teddy bear.

Kaela quickly opened a new window on the internet and found a picture to send to Phoenix.

Phoenix: Cute!

Kaela: But our peach trees do attract monkeys. Our dogs are forever barking at them until the monkeys get annoyed and throw peaches at them. Lakota had a half-rotten peach explode on her the other day. It was disgusting. I didn't even bother bathing her, just took her to the beach to wash it off in the ocean. She loved it.

Phoenix: Hahahaha! I love your African stories. Are you an only child?

Kaela: Yes Ma'am.

Phoenix: Isn't that lonely?

Kaela: No, I enjoy it. Anyway, both my parents have a lot of siblings. So there are a lot of cousins and they don't live very far away. Isn't it hard having six brothers?

Phoenix: It's hard having younger brothers. They are always in my way and under my feet. And just generally being a nuisance. But my older brothers are ace! My twin brother is directing the play that I'm writing. We make a good team, the two of us. And Satyr and Chiron are funny. They always make me laugh. But I guess it is easier to get along with them because they are a bit older and I never really see them, so there is no time to fight.

Kaela: Trix is madly in love with Satyr.

Phoenix: He has a girlfriend.

Kaela: That's okay, she is also madly in love with Chiron.

Phoenix: I'll put in a good word for her.

Kaela: She would die of embarrassment. What

does your mother think of your play?

Phoenix: She loves it. She thinks I need to lay off the 'girl power' thing because she says it might distract the audience from my writing. Maybe she is right. What does yours think of your article?

Kaela: My mom is dead.

Phoenix: Oh man, I'm sorry. That sucks. What happened?

Kaela: We don't know. She went riding one day, and the horse came back without her. They never found her.

Phoenix: That's horrible. So is there always a fear in the back of your mind that horse riding could lead to something so horrible?

Kaela: I suppose. That's why I am always so careful with riding. I take no risks. Stick to what the books say.

Phoenix: That may ruin your fun though. My dad is also dead. He died two years ago.

Kaela: I'm sorry.

Phoenix: One day he got into his car, drove away and we never saw him alive again.

Kaela: That is terrible. I'm so sorry. You guys seem to be doing well though. My family took YEARS to recover.

Kaela wasn't entirely sure that they had recovered.

Phoenix: We weren't to begin with. But we all seem to have pulled together to make life better for ourselves. My big brothers are doing so well in everything, they even help my mom support the family. My twin is taking a college course in directing and he is only in high school. And my grandfather, who is my father's father, is running for Chief. He started the charity to do it in my dad's name, because my dad always wanted to do it, but was too scared to start. My biggest brother (Chiron) is helping him run it. In a way, my dad's death was the best thing for us. Is that sad?

Kaela: No, he gave you a gift.

Phoenix: Thank you. That made me cry a bit. I

can't believe I am confessing this stuff to a stranger on the other side of the world. Isn't that strange?

Kaela: I don't believe in strange. There are no coincidences. We all have the power to do anything we want, but what you need always seems to be handed to you at just the right time.

Phoenix: So you are a gift too?

Kaela thought about the advice Phoenix had given her for the article. It had been sitting in her head for weeks before she had used it to write an article that was above and beyond what she had expected.

A tiny little voice rose to the surface of the murky waters of her brain, a voice that reminded her of Phoenix's ability to admit that life had gone on even without her dad, and even to help her talk about him. It was an ability Kaela refused to adopt. She pushed the voice down. She had neither the heart nor the strength to deal with it.

Kaela: I think you are a gift too.

Trixie used her mobile to go through her LetsChat account. Phoenix had both accepted her friend request, and gone through each of her photos with her usual excited comments. If she was a diabolical ploy to come between Kaela and Trixie, she was a bad one. She seemed just as interested in what Trixie did as what Kaela got up to.

She seemed particularly interested in Trixie's dressage photos.

Phoenix White Feather: *I saw dressage on TV once, I could not wrap my brain around it. It speaks about your talent that you can do it.*

Trixie stared at the comment, "Yes, this woman is definitely a ploy to bring my friendship down. Look at her complimenting me and taking an interest in me. Holy Darwin, she is so evil!"

Then she laughed, Kaela would have loved her little sarcastic remark. Now there was no Kaela to laugh, Trixie sat alone and spoke to herself.

What was it they said about talking to yourself, the first sign of insanity?

Well then, apparently, Trixie was well on her way.

"Just don't start answering yourself," she said, "Because that is the second sign of insanity."

It was a hot day, and she was stood under the shade of the oak tree by the fence of the feeding paddock. She spied a collection of riders gathered around the creek that ran through the paddock. She forced herself up and went over.

"There's Trixie, ask her, she'll know," Russell said as she walked over.

"Know what?"

"When the next solar eclipse is," Jane answered.

Trixie stared at her, too shocked to think.

Was the universe truly trying to talk to her? Telling her that astrophysics was the way forward? She didn't believe in signs and portents (or at least, not out loud), so she could only assume it was all a coincidence.

"Um, I remember reading that there will be a partial solar eclipse later this year. You won't be able to see it with the naked eye, but I'll show you a little trick to see it."

"Yay!" the three little riders cried.

Russell sat on the trunk of the fallen tree, his booted feet swinging back and forth, dangling above the water. He smiled at her, and she quickly looked away.

"What are you guys doing here?"

"We are looking at the bushbabies," Amy said, and pointed up.

Trixie looked up into the overhanging trees. Little furry creatures scuttled across the branches, their big eyes taking up most of their faces, their ears nearly bigger than their heads. Trixie had always loved bushbabies, they reminded her of a stuffed toy her father had once won at a funfair. "Here, have it," her father had said and given it to her, "It looks like a fluffed up version of a squirrel."

That was exactly how Trixie saw bushbabies, fluffed up versions of squirrels.

Kaela was the only one who agreed.

Trixie hated fighting with her friend. She had to make up with her.

"I gotta go."

The riders watched her scuttle off.

"Well hello there, Wawa," Leo Willoughby said as Kaela entered the kitchen.

"Hi, Dad,"

"Why aren't you at the stable?"

"Writing my article."

"Did you get it done?"

Kaela nodded, and looked at the secret hiding place at the back of the pantry. There were chocolate biscuits in there. But with her father sitting at the counter, she could hardly bring them out now. Not unless she wanted an hour-long lecture. She sighed and took out a jar of olives instead. She struggled to open it until her father took it off her and, with one easy twist, he removed the lid. Kaela hated it when he did that. It made her feel incapable of sorting her own life out.

"Dad, I forgot to ask Uncle Owen if we could borrow some chairs from the restaurant. I need them for the show jumping competition."

"So phone him now and ask him."

Kaela shrugged, "It's such late notice that I think he'll be mad."

"You should have asked sooner then."

"I know," she conceded, and popped an olive in her mouth.

"Don't worry little shrub, I'll ask him," he stood up, went to the pantry, pulled out the secret biscuits and gave them to her, "Does that make you feel better?"

She stared at the biscuits in shock: now she would have to find a new hiding place, "Thank you."

"So why don't you look happy?"

Kaela shrugged and wolfed down two biscuits, they tasted better than the olives (especially since they didn't come with a lecture), "Lots on my mind."

"Such as?"

Her father also acted as a counsellor to his patients, he sometimes forgot to leave that part of him at the office.

"Do you think that it is more important to know information than have the ability to do it?"

"I think they are both important."

"What happens if I know all this different information on how to do complicated riding, but I struggle to put that into practice?"

"As long as you are having fun with riding, then that's all that matters."

"But isn't it hypocritical to have the info, and not be able to do anything with it?"

Leo shrugged and tucked a long strand of hair behind his ear. Kaela inwardly laughed at the rebel in her father – his English mother had raised him on the myth of their family being related to Celtic warriors. Kaela thought he might still be living by that. His shoulder-length brown hair hadn't been cut any shorter for as long as Kaela could remember … He wasn't what you expected, particularly for his patients. She liked that. He was a good role model.

"When I am struggling with a patient and everything I have tried has not worked, I get hold of my old lecturers and ask them for advice. Without fail, every time I've done this, they have given me advice that, firstly, works, but that is also something I would have never even thought of."

"What does that have to do with riding?"

"I'm showing you that there will always be someone who has more knowledge in their head, than the will to do something with it. You are amazing at history, do you want to be a historian?"

"No."

"Yet you have that information in your head if you need it."

"I guess."

"Well, I wanted to do something with my knowledge besides give it to someone else. That is why I *practise* homeopathy, but the people I run to in times of trouble, *teach* it. There are keepers of knowledge, and the users of it. Understand?"

Kaela nodded and ate another biscuit.

"What do you think of the idea that if I don't make it as an author, then I have a riding school and I teach?"

Leo looked at her, heavy rain clouds dominated the sky behind him, "Why can't you do both?"

A universe of possibilities opened up in front of her. Why had she never thought that she could be both writer and riding teacher?

"Thanks, Dad. Good advice. You are also a keeper of knowledge."

"I try," he smiled and grabbed the last biscuit before she could.

Kaela thought about all she had to tell Trixie, then she thought about the fight they had. She sighed loudly.

"Why are you still sad?"

"Got into a fight with Trixie today."

"Well I just saw her walk past the gate, go sort it out," Leo said, and pointed to the brown gate at the end of their driveway.

Kaela rushed past her father and ran out the house, through the gate and down the road. Trixie didn't need to pass the house on her way home. Kaela hoped this meant that she wanted to resolve this fight too.

"Trixie!" Kaela called.

The girl on her bike stopped and turned. For a moment, Kaela thought that the girl on the bike wasn't Trixie at all, and she was running down the road for no reason.

"You left the gate open," Trixie said, and pointed.

Kaela looked behind her and sure enough, Lakota and

Breeze were careening towards her at top speed. Both girls grabbed a dog as they bolted past.

"I'm sorry for yelling at you," Kaela cried breathlessly. "You were right. I took on way too much. I'm not superwoman. And because I took on so many things *everything* suffered."

"Well not everything, you did a good job teaching the little ones. I couldn't have done that."

"Well, yeah but you still had to tack up Quiet Fire and find my stuff, so all that got stuffed up."

"I'm sorry I insulted the writing course. I know it is important to you. I just think that maybe it is too important. Whether you go there or not, you're still good enough. I think you are making a chore out of something you love, for people who aren't worth it."

"Maybe you're right. But I still want to *try*. I'm sorry I didn't take your struggles with the subjects seriously. I think you are being really clever in choosing your subjects so that you still have choices later on."

Trixie shrugged, "If I am going to be honest, there are only two directions I want to go. And both of those directions mean computer science is redundant. I think I'm going to scrap that idea."

"And even if you change your mind, you can always just change your subjects."

Trixie nodded and handed Breeze over, Kaela quickly grabbed at her collar.

"I'm sorry for not helping out when I knew you were

struggling. I should have reminded you about the chairs sooner. And the microphone."

Kaela's stomach dropped. She groaned and stomped her foot – another thing to slip her mind!

"Don't worry about it," Trixie said with a wave of her hand, "I spoke to Bart and he's sorting it out."

Jealousy kicked at Kaela.

"You were speaking to Bart?"

"Yes, he's sad. I think he misses his mother. She has been gone for ages."

The dogs began tugging for freedom, "I have to get them inside," said Kaela.

"Well I have to get home. I forgot my great-gran is coming for dinner."

"Oh, a whole night of talking about Georgian pearls."

"I do not understand that woman's obsession with pearls. They aren't even precious or semi-precious stones. And why Georgian? She was not around in Georgian times!" Trixie cried in exasperation.

"Are you sure?" Kaela said cheekily. "She has an *awful* lot of wrinkles."

Lakota and Breeze howled their support. All the dogs on the road howled their support to the malamutes.

Trixie laughed and got back on her bike.

The girls parted ways just as the rain began. Sweet and soft, cooling the hot land.

❧ Nine ❧

The Friday before the competition was spent prepping. In an act of contrition, Trixie took over teaching duties, and Kaela chose to take advantage of her very rare free time.

She led Quiet Fire into the lunging ring and practised with him. She was so caught up in her own actions, that she failed to notice the uniform clad figure that had walked up to the fence. He stood watching her for a minute before speaking.

"Try a bigger circle," he called out.

Kaela halted Quiet Fire, swung around in the saddle, and looked with shock at Bart.

"Try it with a bigger circle so that Quiet Fire's body is not so curved," he repeated.

Kaela followed his advice; she took Quiet Fire around the length of the lunging ring. She shortened up her inside rein, placed her outside leg behind the girth and continued posting. Quiet Fire was more or less straight, so she could easily find her seat and keep a perfect position.

"That's great. Now spiral inwards, making the circle smaller and smaller, and don't lose that position," Bart called to her. He was stood up on the first rung of the fence now, leaning in and pointing round and round to show what he meant.

She did as she was instructed. She understood the principle of what Bart was saying. If Quiet Fire started with a big circle, she could easily position her body in the correct way. Once he was on a smaller, tighter circle, it would mean that his body was curved in a C shape. If she had positioned herself before he got to that C shape, then she wouldn't have to do it on the tighter circle and most surely get it wrong. If she could do this, then that would mean she had found a way to succeed at ballerina dancing on horseback.

She gave a gentle tug at her inside rein, and pushed inwards with her inside leg. Quiet Fire went slightly to the right. Because the movement was so small, she comfortably kept her position. She held Quiet Fire in that circle until she reached the point where she had changed; there she repeated her former act. She had the same reaction. Kaela did it twice more before she reached the circle that had been giving her so much grief. By now, her adrenalin was pumping, she was completely in focus, she knew she would get it right. She gave a small tug at the rein, pushed her leg in, and held her position. She had it. She trotted comfortably around her

mini circle in the correct position. Even Quiet Fire picked up on her bliss: he gave a little jump in the air, which under normal circumstances would have unsettled her, but this time her legs held her in place. She brought him to a stop, and wrapped her arms around his neck.

"We did it my boy, we did it!" she cried into his mane.

"Well done," Bart said.

But Kaela didn't hear him. She was lost in her own achievement.

Oddly enough, the intermediate class was dedicated to jumping rather than impulsion control.

"Just as I master it. Typical!" Kaela frowned.

Trixie laughed, "Such is life, I suppose."

By the time the class was over, Trixie was grateful to get out of the saddle. Jumping was not her favourite thing. She didn't see the point of it. Why make the horse jump, when you can make him dance? Trixie had also noticed that Kaela had had just as hard a time. Quiet Fire was an excellent jumper, but he wasn't that fond of jumping and on some days made it difficult. Today was one of those days. He had refused a jump twice, nearly throwing Kaela the second time.

"How about 'David's' for dinner?" Trixie called as Kaela hobbled past.

"Sounds like a plan," she called back.

Chinese food would go down nicely.

"It's my turn to pay, remember?" Trixie smiled.

"How come you're so rich all of a sudden?"

"I washed my dad's and mom's cars," Trixie said with pride.

"Can I come?" Bart asked from behind the girls.

"Me too," Russell said.

"Why don't we all go?" Emily, another rider from the intermediate level, asked.

The rest of the riders agreed.

And that was how the intermediate riders from Apley Towers (minus Bella but plus Bart) spent the evening at 'David's'. They all tried something new, including Kaela and Trixie, and they all had a fabulous time. All except David that is – he panicked at the amount of teenagers who had descended on his restaurant. His long-held habit of drinking gallons of English tea in times of stress kept him in the kitchen for most of the night. His Chinese ancestors were probably not all that impressed with his choice of beverage. He even turned Buddha to face the wall.

Only Trixie noticed any of this.

PWF: *I have writer's block. At this rate, Bellatrix will never be saved.*

Trixie frowned at that status.

She could see that Phoenix was online. She clicked on her name and typed a quick message.

Trixie: Bellatrix? The star?

Phoenix: Yes, the star. My play is called 'Battle for Bellatrix'.

Trixie: Why battle? What's happened to it?

Phoenix: It has run out of hydrogen fuel so it is about to die, my lead character jump-starts it and has it run on artificial energy.

Trixie: How? You would need masses of energy, and nothing we have invented on earth would be able to support a star. What did you come up with?

Phoenix: A black hole.

Trixie sat back against the dining room chair in surprise. Phoenix obviously knew quite a bit about space science: when a star dies, a black hole is created, and a black hole has enough energy to destroy light. Of course, the idea that you could harness the energy of a black hole in order to run a star was absolutely ludicrous, not to mention that a black hole was created only after the death of a star. But that was why it was called Science Fiction: it didn't matter that it couldn't actually be done; as long as you used science to create the plot and sort the problems, then it was worthy of praise.

Trixie: WOW! That should be a movie.

Phoenix: Hopefully one day.

Trixie: But Bellatrix is FAR. How does she travel there in only one lifetime?

Phoenix: An Einstein-Rosen bridge.

Trixie's jaw dropped. Phoenix knew the official name of a wormhole in space. She put her hands up to her face and shook her head. If she could high five Phoenix right now, she would.

Trixie: I am keeping my fingers crossed that 'Battle for Bellatrix' becomes a movie. I would be there, front row, opening night. That is beyond awesome. How do you know all this stuff?

Phoenix: Research.

Trixie: I'm applauding you over here.

Phoenix: Yeah well, at this rate, no one is ever going to applaud this play.

Trixie: Why?

Phoenix: How exactly are they going to not only 'capture' the black hole, but place it in the star?

Trixie leaned back and put her hair above her head, "Hmmmmm."

She went through all her knowledge of black holes and stars. Frankly, it boggled her brain.

Trixie: How about they somehow make their spaceship a magnet, and therefore it pushes the black hole towards Bellatrix?

Phoenix: YES!

Trixie: And so the black hole creates energy, and forces the hydrogen gas inside the star out of the way.

Phoenix: Like a fan does to smoke.

155

Trixie: Exactly. That way, the black hole can 'plug' itself into the star and energise it.

Phoenix: AMAZING! Thank you! I'm going to write that right now.

Trixie: There is only one problem with that.

Phoenix: What is that?

Trixie: As soon as the black hole jump-starts Bellatrix, the spaceship will be pulled into the star's gravitational field and be destroyed.

Phoenix: Oh that is simple. When they pushed the black hole towards the star, they also pushed the spaceship backwards into the Einstein-Rosen bridge and it was quickly sucked back to Earth, or at least our solar system.

Trixie: But then they don't get to see Bellatrix come alive again.

Phoenix: Such is life.

Trixie laughed, she loved that saying, it was one of her favourites. She smiled at the conversation and looked up.

And screamed.

"Monkey! Monkey inside! Dad! Dad! Where are you? There is a monkey inside."

"Just give him a bar of soap and leave him be," her father called from the lounge.

Trixie angled herself against the wall and scooted across the room and into the kitchen. She grabbed a banana, returned to the dining room, and waved it in front of the monkey. His eyes locked onto the curved yellow fruit. Trixie threw it out the open sliding door. The monkey dived after it. Trixie ran forward and shut the door.

Trixie: There was a monkey in the house. Had to get him out. Threw a banana. Father didn't come to the rescue. Had to save myself. See if he gets a Father's Day present this year.

Phoenix: Man, I love these African stories!!!

✒ Ten ✒

On the day of Apley Towers' first ever internal show jumping competition, the stable was abuzz with activity.

"Wow. You'd think this was an international competition or something," Trixie said.

Trixie had a point: from the amount of spectators gathering in front of the ring, you would never think that only eight little girls were competing.

The course stood in the beginners' ring, while the intermediate ring hosted only the cross jump. Russell, Bart and Derrick had built the course while the beginners had groomed, cleaned and tacked. Kaela and Trixie had set the chairs up – chairs that were graciously, if not grumpily, provided by Kaela's Uncle Owen. The grooms cleaned the paddock and started the fire for the barbecue.

By twelve o'clock, the show was set to start.

Kaela took a quick trip around the stable. She was proud

of what she saw. The white chairs faced the beginners' ring in seven neat rows. They looked slightly out of place in the dust and dirt of Apley. Hopefully the parents wouldn't notice such delicate intricacies. The barbecue was blazing and ready for cooking. Cooler boxes and picnic baskets littered the paddock, filled with drinks and food. Kaela's stomach grumbled as she thought of the potatoes waiting to be baked. She took an errant stick over to the fire and threw it in.

"Careful there," Joseph said.

"I will be."

The wind blew through the trees, swaying them to a music only they could hear. Kaela looked around the paddock, trying to imagine the land before there was any of this here, before the Europeans and the Native tribes. If she was quiet enough, she could hear the heartbeat of the land.

"Maybe you have to be still to see things clearly," Joseph said and walked off.

Kaela watched him until he disappeared behind the stalls.

"What exactly do I need to see clearly?"

For some reason, Neverland popped into her head. She thought of the Lost Boys: they had been taken to Neverland to live, parentless, for the rest of their lives. It didn't matter that there were no adults to care for them, they cared for each other.

Kaela watched as the older riders rushed about, helping the younger riders. At Apley Towers, they cared for each other too.

The first of the parents had begun to arrive. Kaela could hear Jeremy stomping around in a nursing stall. He had to be locked up, or he would attack the cars. He wasn't too pleased.

Kaela threw one more stick into the fire, and walked towards the rings.

The competition beckoned.

"Good afternoon Ladies and Gentlemen, and welcome to Apley Towers. We hope you enjoy the show today," Kaela said into a microphone that Bart's friend had been kind enough to set up for them. "My name is Kaela Willoughby, and I will be the host as well as the judge. The other four judges are Beatrix King, Russell Drover, Bartholomew Oberon and Derrick Drummer."

"Our first competition is a horse and rider presentation," Trixie said speaking into her own microphone. "Here the rider will be judged on their own appearance as well as the appearance of their horse."

"Could the riders please enter the ring as they are called?" Kaela said.

"Amy Hanscom, with Caesar."

Amy walked into the ring, and led Caesar to the position she had been shown the day before. There was small applause from the audience.

"Samantha Everette, with Apache."

Samantha walked into the ring leading the stable's famous piebald; she stopped right next to Amy.

Once all girls were in the ring, the judges began circling. Kaela, Trixie and Russell were each given only one rider to look over, while Bart took two and Derrick took three. They had checklists that they had to work from in order to mark their riders. Kaela walked over to Rebecca with the checklist. The girls had been told to stand up straight next to their horses. Kaela looked Rebecca up and down. There did not have to be complete silence between judge and rider, but Kaela didn't feel like talking and Rebecca seemed too nervous to start a conversation.

The judge had to check that the competitor had done as she had been instructed. Her brown hair was neatly tucked away in a bun, Kaela checked that off. She was wearing the correct clothes as well as shoes, hard hat, and chaps. Rebecca had passed her presentation, but that was the easy part, riders almost always passed without a problem. The dilemma came when the judges exercised the tricks on the tack. You had to be able to get a finger between the throat-lash and the horse itself. Kaela could not. The bit guards had to be placed comfortably against the horse's lips. The bit guards had been put in such a position that they seemed to be pulling Rhapsody's lips into a smile. Kaela fixed them; Rhapsody's ears automatically went forward. Kaela moved onto the saddle, she grabbed the stirrup and pushed down as hard as she could. Down came the saddle.

"Oh no," Rebecca cried.

"Don't worry, it happened to me too," Kaela said comfortingly. She put everything on the floor, undid Rhapsody's girth and resaddled him.

"Good as new," Kaela said with a smile.

Rebecca's eyes were filled with tears, "Am I disqualified?"

"I would never disqualify the first person brave enough to put the bit in her mouth," Kaela said.

Rebecca smiled broadly, showing the gaps where her front teeth used to be.

The judges followed the common procedure of awarding ribbons after each event. The five did quick calculations to see which rider had made the least mistakes.

"Okay, well we have come up with the three winners," Kaela said into the microphone. "In third place is Amy Hanscom with Caesar."

There was applause and yelling from the audience, Trixie went forward to put the rosette on Caesar's bridle. Kaela liked the ribbons: they were all blue with first, second or third stamped in gold on one of the streamers. And in the centre, on white cardboard, was the golden face of a horse with the wind blowing through the mane. Apley Towers was written in gold beneath the horse. Yvonne had gone all out for these ribbons.

"In second place is Shanaeda Mohamed with Star," the same reaction.

"In first place, the rider and horse that were best presented, is Kirsten Matthews on Flight."

There was more applause for the three winners.

"If the riders would kindly make their exit and warm up their horses, we will continue with the form jumping competition." Kaela said.

Eight little girls turned to the left and walked out the ring. The rosettes were waved proudly by the winners. Star seemed to know he was better looking; he was actually prancing out of the ring.

Once the horses were warm, the form competition began.

"In this competition, the rider is judged on their form as they go over the jump," Trixie said. "The jump is twelve centimetres high and is a cross jump. The jump requires more skill than the normal bar jump."

Once again Amy was first, she jumped without a problem. Seven girls followed in the same fashion. The judges had decided that only a few things would be judged, and not the form all together. Were their heels down? Were they gripping with their calves? Did they go down at the right time? Did they come into the jump straight? And most importantly, did they hang onto the mane, false martingale or pommel? Because all eight girls jumped without a hitch, the decision came down to who looked better.

"Well done girls, you all did very well, but unfortunately there can only be three winners," Kaela nearly dropped the microphone in horror, she could not believe she had just said that; she had always detested that saying.

"And in third place we have Michelle Baron on Pumbaa,"

Kaela was having a hard time believing that Michelle actually got Pumbaa over the jump without putting carrots on the other side of it. She deserved first place for that.

"In second place is Danielle Marq with Sun Dancer."

Danielle clapped along with the audience, Kaela could only laugh.

"And in first place, and this rider truly is an exceptional jumper for her age, Shanaeda Mohamed on Star."

An entire row of people on the front row stood up and cheered for Shanaeda.

"Wow, I wish I had that much support when I won my first ribbon," Russell said.

"The three winners may take a victory trot around the ring," Kaela said.

By the time the riders had left the ring, the parents began to get nervous: now was the time for the real danger. Kaela looked over her shoulder at the course, it was set up so that the rider would have to make a U shape. The first two jumps were in a straight line, the rider would then have to bring the horse around to jump the next two.

"The next competition is a course," Trixie said. "The jumps are eight inches high, and as you can see there are four of them. The rider who finishes in the shortest time with no faults is the winner. Knocking a pole is a fault, as well as falling, and refusal to jump. Three refusals results in disqualification, three falls are a disqualification, and leaving the ring without finishing the course is a disqualification."

"Would Danielle Marq, with Sun Dancer, please enter the ring," Kaela said.

Danielle looked nervous but all five judges knew that she was prepared: the beginners had practised this exact course enough times to know it by heart. Danielle put Sun Dancer in the correct position and waited for the bell. Bart rang it and Danielle nudged Sun Dancer into action. The horse trotted to the first jump, popped over and trotted to the next one. Kaela could not help but laugh: they were all making such a big thing out of such a tiny course. The horses did not even need to jump; they could trot over the bars. Kaela was convinced that the horses jumped simply to humour the human riders.

Danielle jumped the second bar, trotted Sun Dancer out a bit, and then turned the mare around. The action looked clumsy, Kaela knew that was because Danielle was not practising impulsion control and was simply letting the horse do as she pleased. Sun Dancer trotted to the first jump, took it like the pro jumper she was, and trotted to the next one. Once Danielle had done all four jumps, she brought the horse to a stop. Loud applause erupted from the crowd. Horse and rider left the ring beaming.

One by one the riders took the course, and one by one they completed it without fault. It was only Jane who had trouble on the course. She did the course at a fast trot. Jinx was at the first jump before Jane was ready for it; he took the second jump while Jane was recovering from the first jump. In her rush, Jane turned him too soon, and Jinx refused the jump.

"One fault for Jane James," Derrick said over the microphone. Kaela wished he hadn't said that; it only made the little girl more nervous. To everyone's surprise, Jane handled the situation like a star. She turned Jinx around, walked him to the fence post, turned him back around, and nudged him into a slow trot; she took the last two jumps perfectly. Jane received more applause than any of the other riders had.

"Although it was difficult to pick winners, we have eventually come up with three," Kaela said. "In third place, with a time of 31.6 seconds and no faults, Kirsten Matthews on Flight."

Kirsten came forward with her traditional smug look, but Kaela was too proud of the girls to let it bother her.

"In second place, with a time of 31.2 seconds and no faults, is Rebecca Foster on Rhapsody."

Rhapsody looked around at the crowd as though they were applauding him.

"And in first place, with a time of 29.8 seconds and no faults, is Shanaeda Mohamed on Star."

For the second time that day, Star pranced out of the ring.

"The next course is made up of six jumps. All the same rules apply," Trixie said.

Two more jumps had been added to the course, the rider now had to bring their horse around a second time to do the last two jumps.

Kirsten was the first to jump this time, she took a slow trot and managed the course without fault. Next came Rebecca,

Shanaeda, Jane, Michelle, Danielle, and then Amy. Samantha was last to ride.

She led Apache to the starting position and waited for the bell, when it went she nudged Apache into a trot. It was a slow, comfortable trot and Samantha took the first two jumps with ease. She brought Apache around for the next two, which were done equally well. The problem started when Samantha brought Apache around for the next two jumps, which were placed further apart from each other than the previous two sets had been. Apache took this as an open invitation to canter. He bolted forward, ignoring Samantha's tug at the reins. Samantha was unprepared when he took the first jump – as soon as Apache landed, Samantha jolted in the saddle and her feet lost the stirrups. Apache continued cantering for the next jump; Kaela was certain Samantha was going to fall. Miraculously, four weeks of training came out, Samantha's leg muscles tightened around Apache's side. Apache took the jump, Samantha gripped even harder, and both horse and rider landed comfortably on the other side. Before Samantha had even brought Apache to a stop, the entire crowd was on their feet, applauding the little rider. Even the judges were clapping. Kaela was clapping so hard

that her hands were turning red. Samantha waved to her mother, and then waited for permission to leave the ring. The judges had been so busy applauding they had completely forgotten that the clock was still running. Derrick quickly stopped the timer, subtracted thirty seconds and wrote the number down. Samantha was then free to go. As she exited the ring, Amy, Danielle, Rebecca, Shanaeda, Jane and Michelle all stood up in their stirrups and applauded their brave comrade.

When the crowd had finally quieted down, Kaela stood up and announced the winners.

"In third place, with a time of 53.9 seconds and no faults, is Danielle Marq on Sun Dancer. In second place, with a time of 51.5 seconds and no faults, is Michelle Baron on Pumbaa. And in first place, with a time of 48.2 seconds and no faults, is Shanaeda Mohamed."

All three girls accepted their ribbons to great applause.

"You may take your victory trot around the ring," Kaela said.

Shanaeda turned her trot into a victory canter. With four ribbons, she had the right to do so.

When the crowd calmed down, Kaela announced, "We have two more ribbons to give out today."

"Yes, these last two girls really deserve it," Trixie said.

"For clear thinking under enormous pressure, we award a blue ribbon to Jane James."

Jane smiled a toothless grin at her parents before coming forward.

"Well done Jane," Trixie said as she hooked the ribbon to Jinx's bridle.

"The next ribbon goes to the person who did not panic when in danger, and used her training to save herself. This ribbon is awarded to Samantha Everette for paying attention in class," Kaela said.

Samantha's mother clapped so hard that she nearly knocked over the people next to her, who ducked to avoid her rogue elbows and hands.

"Well done Sammy," Trixie said. She had to stand on tiptoe to put the rosette in Apache's bridle.

"Would you girls like to take a victory trot?" Kaela asked.

"As long as it is just a trot," Samantha answered.

Kaela watched as the two girls trotted around the ring to a standing ovation.

"Would all the competitors take a victory lap? You all deserve it," Kaela said.

Trixie and Kaela watched as eight little riders on five fat ponies and three big horses trotted around the ring.

Derrick asked for the microphone and addressed the girls, "Well done beginners. You have made us all proud. But I want you to remember that riding is about enjoyment."

Both Kaela and Trixie's ears perked up.

"And remember, you will always be the best at anything, so long as it makes you happy."

The crowd applauded once again.

"Lastly, I would like to thank everyone who put any effort into the show. You all know who you are. But I especially want to thank Trixie and Kaela. They pretty much pulled this thing together on their own. Let's give them a round of applause."

The crowd did.

"Though they are little, they are fierce."

Kaela raised her eyebrows at Derrick. *'Shakespeare'* – she mouthed. He grinned back at her.

"You see, writers rule the world, we are everywhere," Kaela said.

Trixie rolled her eyes and groaned. Russell laughed and cheered the girls (this made Trixie groan more).

"So was it worth all the time and energy we put into it?" Trixie asked.

"Yes, it was!" Kaela exclaimed with pride.

"So what are we going to do next?" Trixie asked.

Kaela turned to look at her friend; both girls had mischievous smiles plastered on their faces, "Well, *The Primary Blab* gets released on Monday. There is always that to look forward to."

❧ Eleven ❧

Just as Kaela and Tess had predicted, Bella had known the article was written about her. She had spent the majority of the day scowling at the two, until riders from Apley and its rival stables also began to assume that Bella was the inspiration, thanks to her infamously lazy antics. This seemed to jolt Bella a bit. Being in the midst of a battle with Kaela was one thing, but being called 'lazy' and 'cruel' by other riders seemed to be opening her eyes to the realities of her responsibilities. Kaela looked around at the people in the corridors who were reading her newspaper; both her article and the articles she had edited. She felt quite proud of the way that her words sat between the fingers of her fellow students. She caught a glimpse of the article on the cover of the newspaper. The headline said 'Ten Ways to Earn your Animal's Love', and the photo, in black and white, stood proudly next to the actual article. Kaela laughed despite

herself. At that moment, more than any other, Kaela realised that through words she was able to touch the lives of other people. While sitting there on the steps, a moment of calm in a torrent of school kids, it all came to her. She knew she would not have to worry about whether or not she got onto the writing course. She knew that she was talented and dedicated enough to get by, with or without their tutoring.

She just had to trust herself and do the best she could.

A boy from her class waved to her, she waved back. He held up the newspaper, pointed to the article and gave a thumbs up. At that moment, Kaela knew that she had done what she'd set out to do. She had tried, and that was good enough for her. She was fine with that. A tutorship from J.M. Barrie Writing School would be a nice little titbit to show off, but she was strong from the inside.

And that was enough.

Riding made her happy, teaching made her happy too.

And, as long as she was happy, she was doing something right.

Trixie packed the last of her books in her backpack as the final bell of the day went off. A loose page fell from her file and see-sawed to the floor. She looked at it closely. It was the list of subjects she had written. She scrunched it up and threw it in the recycle bin. The subjects only had to be chosen in August. She wasn't going to worry about it until then, if she was going to worry about it at all.

For all she knew, she would change her mind and become a cowboy or a florist.

She zipped up her backpack and sauntered down the school corridor, smiling to herself. If she got home as quickly as possible, she could then get to the stable sooner and spend more time with the horses.

For the moment, riding made her happy, and as long as she was happy, she was doing something right.

When Kaela walked into the stables later that afternoon, she almost dropped dead at the sight. Bella had KaPoe on cross ties and was vigorously grooming him. Behind her, propped on a chair, was spotless tack and, more importantly, a sparkling saddle blanket.

"She even mucked out her own stall," Derrick whispered as he walked past, "we have no idea what is going on but we are all terrified."

Kaela smiled at herself; she knew what was going on, and she was happy that Bella had pulled her act together. She just hoped it would stay that way.

The stable was a hive of activity, as it always was. Grooms running, horses and children all over the place, and in the beginners' ring stood Wendy teaching the little ones. There was something slightly morose about that. After four weeks of teaching them, it was bittersweet to have to hand them back.

They trotted around Wendy, their legs strong and their heels down.

Kaela puffed with pride.

With that, she turned around and walked towards the stables, her favourite place in the world.

❧ Twelve ❧

"Would someone please tell me what this is about?" Phoenix asked.

"I told you, I would explain during the ceremony," Kaela said to the laptop.

Although it was night and pitch-black outside, through the brilliance of video calling, Kaela could see Phoenix sitting in her kitchen, in bright sunlight.

"Phoenix, am I to assume you brought the intended wares?"

"You assume correctly, my Lady."

"Could you people talk like you are from the twenty-first century please? You're freaking me out," Trixie said and sipped her cream soda.

"Don't drink it yet!" Kaela cried.

"What is it?" Phoenix asked with suspicious eyes on the glass.

"It is cream soda. Awesome drink. Best in the world. This woman," Trixie gestured to Kaela with her eyes, "said I had to bring my favourite drink, so here it is."

"What do you have, and why is it blue?" Phoenix asked Kaela.

"Wheat-grass with blueberries and chia," Kaela said with pride.

"You need to move in with us and control our diets," Phoenix said with big eyes.

"No, trust me. You don't want that," Trixie said and waved her hands for emphasis, "I put two sugars in my tea, and was lectured for an hour."

Lakota howled her support from the ground.

"Keep quiet you mad mutt," Kaela cried. "What do you have to drink?"

"Water," Phoenix said and lifted her glass.

"Boring," Trixie and Kaela cried together.

"Only if you think that dipping my glass into the river that runs through the reservation and is considered sacred, is boring," she said in one breath, and raised her eyebrows.

"That's pretty cool," Kaela said.

"Exactly."

"What did you bring to eat?" Trixie asked.

"Fry bread," Phoenix held up what looked like a mass of fried dough. "Ma makes it. What did you bring?"

"Popcorn," Trixie held up the overflowing bowl.

Both girls looked to Kaela.

"Blackberries for vitamin C, lemon to fight off illness – I've been very stressed lately, that's killer to the immune system. Also a spear of asparagus – good for detoxing, I've had restaurant food twice in two weeks. And an avocado. I don't really know what they do but my dad is always recommending them to his patients."

"Hold on, I want to write all that down," Phoenix said.

"Don't you believe in junk food?" Trixie asked with a bored voice.

"There's no such thing. There is either food or junk."

"Wow! You set the bar to impossible heights," Phoenix said.

"Okay, is everyone ready?" Kaela asked.

"Yes," both girls said together.

"So I'll begin," Kaela picked up her notebook and began to read. "From the dawn of time, man – and woman – has needed companions. Somebody to be there for a laugh when times get tough, someone to support you when you have taken on too much," Kaela looked at Trixie. "Someone who comes into your life and thinks you are a gift." she looked at Phoenix. "Or someone to help you with the science in your future award-winning play," Trixie and Phoenix looked at each other. "There is a belief that the Greek Gods made humans with two heads, four arms and four legs. And then separated them into two people."

"Here we go," Trixie rolled her eyes.

"Anyway, they were then doomed to search for their other

179

half. I'm not sure I believe that. I think we were made into a giant person with more heads than we can count, and when we were separated we were left with a memory of those other heads who kept us company. I think that's how we find the people who feel like they're a part of us. And so I raise my glass," Kaela picked up her drink, the other two girls did too, "and salute the two heads who were once joined to my body."

Both girls laughed.

"Cheers," Kaela said and took a sip.

"Cheers," Phoenix and Trixie cried and took sips.

Lakota howled her support, bringing Breeze into the study to join the howl.

Kaela put her drink down and picked her notebook back up.

"When I was little, my mother used to read a book to me called Peter Pan. It still sits on my bedside table, reminding me of her," Kaela resumed reading from her notebook. "In this story there is a band of merry little boys who accompanied Peter Pan on all of his adventures."

"They found Tiger Lily," Phoenix said.

"Exactly. They were little boys who had forgotten what a mother is," Kaela stopped to take a deep breath and swallow the dry lump in her throat, and kept her eyes focused on her notebook, although it didn't have this bit of her speech written down in it. "They had forgotten what a father is," Kaela took a quick look at Phoenix, long enough to see her lower lip slightly tremble. "They had their problems, but they had each other. They were lost, but they were found in each other. They survived because they each belonged to a band of brothers called 'The Lost Boys'."

She paused for a moment.

"We aren't boys, but together we seem to bring out the best in one another. We each make the other strong. So I'm asking the two of you to join my band of unbiological sisters. I call it, *The Lost Kodas*."

"I accept," Phoenix said quickly and loudly, nearly sloshing her glass of water over the screen.

"I second the motion," Trixie grinned.

"Technically you would be third-ing it," Kaela frowned.

"You wanna go in the pool?" Trixie raised her eyebrows and jabbed her thumb over her shoulder to where the pool shimmered in the moonlight through the window.

"Yes, it is quite hot," Kaela laughed.

"I am freezing my butt off over here, and you lot are contemplating the pool," Phoenix said with a shake of her head, making her long, dark hair fall into her face. "There is four feet of snow outside my front door!"

"Snow would be welcomed right now."

"Getting back to the motion," Kaela lifted her asparagus spear.

"Are you going to knight us?" Trixie teased.

"No, I'm waiting for you to pick up your junk."

"Hey, popcorn is not junk," Phoenix cried.

"Are you defending it because Native Americans invented it?"

Phoenix's eyes grew wide, "Really?"

"Yes. How do you not know that?"

"Everyone knows that," Trixie said.

Phoenix turned away from the laptop, "Hey Ma! Natives invented popcorn!"

"You're kidding?" a voice called from somewhere in the house.

"Jeez, this is monumental," Phoenix said.

"Anyway, getting back to the ceremony. Grab your food," the girls did as they were told. "Mistress Phoenix Lily White Feather and Mistress Beatrix Warne King, I hereby invite you to enter into the sacred circle of *The Lost Kodas*. Your duties will be to support the other members, to always be a friend, and to trust that *The Lost Kodas* will always be there for you and look out for your best interests. You may only enter this circle with perfect love and perfect trust, and above all, perfect hope for a better life for us all," she turned to Trixie, "Mistress Beatrix, do you choose to enter *The Lost Kodas*?"

"I do," Trixie said with a smile.

"Welcome to *The Lost Kodas*," Kaela said with a small bow, "you may eat your popcorn."

"And thank a Native for it," Phoenix said.

"Thank you, Phoenix," Trixie raised a handful of popcorn before shoving it in her mouth.

"Mistress White Feather, do you choose to enter *The Lost Kodas*?"

"With pride, I do."

"Welcome to *The Lost Kodas*."

Phoenix ripped off a bit of fry bread and popped it into her mouth.

"Mistress Willoughby," Trixie said, "do you choose to enter *The Lost Kodas*?"

"I do."

"Welcome, then. Eat your vegetables."

"And your lemon," Phoenix said between bites.

"Now Phoenix, tell me exactly which brother is sitting there?" Trixie asked quietly, leaning slightly closer into the screen.

Phoenix swung the laptop around to face a long-haired teenage boy sitting at the kitchen counter with a mountain of books, and a sandwich almost as big as his head. He was left-handed, and held the pen at an odd angle as he quickly scribbled notes down. His right hand kept his hair out of his face. Kaela and Trixie grinned at one another.

"Say hi, Satyr," Phoenix said.

"Hi Satyr," he said without looking up.

"Hey, don't be rude to my friends. They are my missing heads."

Satyr looked up in confusion, "Your missing heads?" he turned away from the laptop and cried into the belly of the house, "Ma! Your daughter has officially lost it."

"I thought so, she's been screaming about popcorn," a voice answered.

"And now she is talking about her missing heads."

"Huh?"

"Yeah, I blame the South Africans, they are on the computer, they are …" Satyr turned back to the laptop to look at Trixie and Kaela. He turned back to his mother, "Hey Ma! I think I've lost my mind. There are South Africans in their pyjamas, eating asparagus."

"Have some fry bread and lie down," his mother answered.

The laptop shifted back to Phoenix, "And that is Satyr," she said with a shake of her head.

The three girls laughed, the dogs howled, and Trixie choked on some popcorn. Kaela pumped her palm hard on her back, which made Lakota jump onto Kaela and knock her down.

"I'd say it was a successful first meeting of *The Lost Kodas*," Trixie said through peals of laughter.

"Definitely," Phoenix said as she put the last of the fry bread in her mouth. "We established that we are all lost Greek heads, Kaela is a health nut who eats blackberries, lemon and asparagus in one meal, popcorn is an invention of my people, and Satyr thinks we're all mad. Kaela then got attacked by her dog, while Trixie nearly choked. All in all, a very successful meeting."

"Hey Ma!" Satyr cried from beyond the rectangle of Phoenix's screen, "I'm going to lie down. These Lost Koda meetings sound dangerous, and I just might be the next target."

"You are a lost koda!" his mother cried.

The three girls laughed, made themselves comfortable and discussed the jumping show, the article, the play, the world.

It was only later that night as Kaela remembered the ceremony that she realised how true her Greek story was. She had found her missing heads. One had been in her life for years, and the other had just joined.

"The Lost Kodas," she said to herself as she fell asleep.

The words slipped off her tongue like a lazy, comfortable creek finding its way through the woods.

Acknowledgements

Firstly, thank you to the team at Sweet Cherry for this opportunity. Thank you all for working so hard on these books, especially Laurie Parsons, who made the books glitter.

Thank you to friends and family (and friends who are family) for all the help and support you gave me while writing this book. I would be lost without all of you.

Thank you to my dad, Anthony King, who read the first story I ever wrote and paid for my riding lessons.

And thank you to Shannon, Kael and Leo. I believe that living with a writer is like living with a bubbling cauldron... only more dangerous. Thank you for risking it and helping me make magic. Thank you for dreaming my dreams with me.

And lastly, thank you to every horse who has ever carried me and taught me to fly.

An interview with Myra King

Where did your main inspiration for Apley Towers come from?

From my own adventures with my riding friends and our stable. Most of what Kaela gets up to, I did at one point in my life.

Did you ride horses when you were a child? Do you still ride now?

I rode for most of my childhood, both in lessons and pleasure riding with friends. I don't ride anymore as I had a serious fall ten years ago and now it is painful to sit in a saddle for a long time.

Did you have a favourite horse when you were younger? Why?

The first horse to show me attitude was a gelding named Pumbaa, but he also rescued me from what would have been a very sticky situation. He was one of the horses to make a massive impact in my life. Quiet Fire was the horse I rode most in lessons and I fell in love with him from the very first moment I laid eyes on him. He was black and beautiful, and carried me as though I was royalty. It was easy to imagine myself in a fantasy novel on his back. Another adorable horse who I'll never forget is a gelding named Jinky. He was a former champion but retired at our stable and was the first horse I ever jumped with. He taught me to fly.

What has been your best riding experience, and your scariest riding experience?

My best riding experience was riding on the beach in Mexico. I love Native American culture and being able to ride on their beach with the tribe, the way they ride, was magic. My scariest riding experience was when I was eleven and I started riding more advanced horses. The jump was put up to 1m, which I had never jumped before, and the horse bolted forward before I was ready. I lost my stirrups and he was cantering far quicker than I was used to so I nearly fell out of the saddle. I had to grip really tightly with my calves. But it was the first time that a horse had to literally launch himself to get over the jump so it was the first time I was aware of the fact that the horse was flying through the air with me on top of him. I had to grip his neck just to stay on, which means I didn't have my reins to stop him. I ended up having to throw myself off to get myself to safety. I must have accidentally told the horse to turn right though, because as soon as I fell, he turned and I landed up underneath him and he had to jump over me. I still have the scar from where his hoof cut me.

What was it like growing up and riding in South Africa?
It was great to have hot weather for most of the year. Our riding lessons were always done in beautiful sunshine and around lots of nature. The thing I enjoyed most about South Africa was the animals. I grew up with the ability to see elephants, lions and leopards in the wild. I can't say I miss the monkeys though; I was always scared of them. They frequently broke into my house and stole my soap.

How do you come up with all of the different characters in the books?
Some of the characters are based on my friends. A lot of the characters are different facets of my own personality. But a few of them came to me on their own.

Do you have any strange writing habits?
I sometimes have to walk around speaking the character's dialogue out loud. The neighbors know me as the mad writer who holds entire conversations with herself.

Do you have any tips or advice for aspiring writers?
Pay close attention to the world and write about it as much as you can.

Do you have any plans to write more books after Apley Towers?
I'm always writing something.

Coming soon in the series...

Book Four

ISBN: 978-1-78226-280-0

Book Five

ISBN: 978-1-78226-281-7

Book Six

ISBN: 978-1-78226-282-4

Pre-order yours today!